Natalie's voice was polite and distant

"Is this a social visit?"

"My dear—*no*," Simone denied haughtily. "Surely you've guessed why I'm here?"

"On the contrary," Natalie answered. "Get whatever it is off your chest. Then leave!"

The other woman gave a high-pitched laugh that sounded faintly off-key. "It's relatively simple. I want Ryan."

"Does Ryan want you?"

Simone's eyes gleamed with a mixture of molten fire and ice. "You have *nothing* compared to what I could give him."

"Except maybe love," Natalie said with quiet conviction, and for a moment she looked incredibly sad.

"Rubbish! I can take Ryan from you as easily as that." Simone clicked her fingers in the air with a decisive snap.

Books by Helen Bianchin

HARLEQUIN PRESENTS

HARLEQUIN ROMANCES

These books may be available at your local bookseller.

For a free catalog listing all titles currently available,
send your name and address to:

Harlequin Reader Service
P.O. Box 52040, Phoenix, AZ 85072-2040
Canadian address: Stratford, Ontario N5A 6W2

HELEN BIANCHIN

yesterday's shadow

Harlequin Books

TORONTO • NEW YORK • LONDON
AMSTERDAM • PARIS • SYDNEY • HAMBURG
STOCKHOLM • ATHENS • TOKYO • MILAN

Harlequin Presents first edition June 1984
ISBN 0-373-10695-5

Original hardcover edition published in 1984
by Mills & Boon Limited

CHAPTER ONE

THE sun was a distant glowing orb in an azure sky, with none of its promised heat evident at this relatively early morning hour.

Natalie leaned back against the cushioned headrest and endeavoured to conjure some interest in the panoramic vista beyond the smoke-tinted window as the bus eased on to the Gold Coast highway at Southport and began its smooth run towards the centre of Surfer's Paradise.

This coastal stretch of south-east Queensland was truly golden, with sand the colour of clover honey. High-rolling waves crashed to its shores in spuming magnificence, providing sought-after surfing conditions, which, coupled with record sunshine hours, brought an abundance of tourists and holidaymakers throughout the year. Innumerable towering high-rise buildings lined the foreshore, bearing evocative names that stirred the imagination and tempted an alternative lifestyle.

With an impartial, slightly jaundiced eye, Natalie observed the changes that had taken place during her three-year absence. Many of the houses along the highway had gone, and in their place stood modern architecturally-designed high-rise that added to a rapidly growing concrete jungle.

The faint hiss of hydraulic brakes coupled with the driver's announcement of arrival prompted Natalie to her feet, and she joined the general exodus of alighting passengers.

A quick glance at her watch confirmed that she would have time for a much-needed cup of coffee.

It had been hours since she had checked out of the hotel in Brisbane, and her stomach demanded sustenance even though her nerves screamed rejection.

The decision to return had taken considerable courage, and for the umpteenth time she damned fate for being so cruel. A slow gnawing fear manifested itself and played havoc with her composure. Given a choice, she would gladly have opted out of the whole wretched scheme— but there was no choice. It was a case of 'damned if you do, damned if you don't'! she conceded wryly. Like it or not—and she didn't, not at *all* —she was committed to confronting a man she had vowed never to have anything to do with for the rest of her life. All her instincts screamed for her to escape while she could, and only determined resolve forced her into a nearby coffee lounge, where she ordered coffee and a light snack.

'Are you on holiday?'

Natalie glanced up as the young waiter placed the food before her. 'No,' she disclaimed shortly, directing him an icy glare from smoky-grey eyes. Heaven preserve her from a self-assured male on the make!

'Would you like cream for the cappucino?' He was persistent, his smile openly speculative as dark Latin eyes, liquid with admiration, roved slowly over her delectable curves.

'No—nor do I need anything else.' She spoke with deceptive softness, but her meaning was unmistakable, and with a philosophical shrug he moved away.

The coffee was aromatic, and she sipped it appreciatively, aware of a soothing effect which, coupled with a serving of toasted bacon and cheese fingers, calmed her digestive juices and helped bolster her morale.

A few minutes after nine o'clock she emerged into the morning sunshine and turned towards the main street. The office building she sought lay three blocks distant, and she deliberately set a brisk pace, oblivious to the frank admiring glances her diminutive five-feet-three-inch form received.

Slim, with curves in all the right places, she possessed an enviable peaches-and-cream complexion that moulded a delicate bone structure. Eyes that lightened or darkened with each change of mood were an intriguing feature, and were fringed with thick dark lashes. Long shoulder-length blonde hair resembling liquid silk shot with streaks of gold owed nothing to artifice and swung softly with every move she made.

A slight breeze tempered the sun's warmth as she crossed the street, zig-zagging her way between traffic, and on reaching the pavement she paused momentarily to draw a calming breath. Ahead of her lay the towering edifice housing the offices of Marshall Associates, and with a glint of defiance she moved towards the electronically-controlled glass doors.

The elegant marble façade echoed the luxuriously appointed interior, its design and décor a visual masterpiece, and she experienced a sense of icy fatalism as she crossed the foyer and entered the elevator. Selecting the appropriate button, she jabbed it with unnecessary force, and was immediately transported with swift precision to her designated level.

Heaven help her, she had *arrived*! Celestial assistance was never more warranted, she decided grimly, and summoning her features into a cool polite mask she crossed the thick-piled carpet towards reception.

'Mr Marshall, please.' Her voice held clipped detachment, and she met the receptionist's quick assessing stare with equanimity.

'May I have your name?'

'Maclean—Natalie Maclean,' she responded evenly, and her stomach muscles tightened as the girl picked up an inter-office phone. If Ryan Marshall refused to see her, her task would be made doubly difficult.

'Mr Marshall has several appointments this morning,' the young girl related efficiently. 'However, there's a possibility that he can fit you in around midday. Will that be suitable?'

The reprieve couldn't be ignored, and Natalie inclined her head in silent acquiescence. She had come too far to wreck whatever chance she had by demanding instant attention. 'Thank you.'

Her self-confidence descended to an all-time low as she turned and walked towards the elevator. Dear God, three hours to fill in!

On reaching the ground level she stepped out into the warm sunshine with no definite purpose in mind. There were not a great number of people around at this relatively early hour as March was not a peak tourist season, and she wandered idly window-shopping, explored a new arcade, then entered a new complex where she spent her time leisurely browsing in several exclusive boutiques. With a further hour until midday, she purchased the daily newspaper and thoroughly scanned its pages over coffee.

It was five minutes to twelve when Natalie presented herself at the reception desk, and this time she was directed to a sumptuously furnished lounge with views over the Nerang River.

'Please take a seat. Mr Marshall shouldn't be long.'

Natalie selected a velvet-upholstered sofa positioned near an expanse of plate-glass. Every minute seemed an hour, despite the wide variety of magazines provided, and the slightest sound succeeded in sending her stomach into a series of painful somersaults.

'Miss Maclean? If you would care to come with me, Mr Marshall will see you now.' The smile was perfunctory, and Natalie stood to her feet, dazed by the effort it took to control her wayward nerves.

Marshall—she hated the name, almost as much as she hated the man who bore it.

Her entire respiratory system seemed out of control, making breathing difficult as she followed in the secretary's wake, and each step taken down that long carpeted corridor seemed to accelerate her inner tension.

'Miss Maclean.' The announcement was professionally delivered, and with the actions of an automaton Natalie moved into the room, hardly aware of the almost silent click of the door as it closed behind her.

Like a magnet her eyes swept to the tall frame positioned indolently at ease behind a central executive desk. Three years had wrought little change—if anything he appeared more dynamic than ever. Broad shoulders tapering to slim taut hips exuded leashed strength beneath casual yet elegantly tailored attire, and there was a rugged, almost animalistic sense of power—an inherent vitality, that was unequalled. Thick, well-groomed light-brown hair held no hint of grey, and the dark golden, almost tigerish, eyes wore an expression of deliberate insolence as they subjected her to a slow encompassing appraisal.

'*Maclean?*' Ryan Marshall taunted with dangerous softness, and Natalie felt an unaccustomed
frisson of fear slither its way down her spine.

'It is my name,' she managed with deceptive
calmness, and saw the edge of his mouth twist with
sardonic cruelty.

'I seem to recall you acquired another.'

She swallowed with difficulty, feeling intensely
vulnerable—*exposed*, beneath the intense, almost
electric masculinity the man projected. It took
incredible effort to instil a semblance of steadiness
into her voice. 'That's something I try very hard to
forget.'

One dark eyebrow rose in wry cynicism. 'Are
you successful?'

No, *damn* you! she wanted to scream. She had
spent too many wakeful nights remembering to
ever be able to forget. Aloud, she indicated with
infinite civility, 'I don't want to take up too much
of your valuable time.'

He shifted slightly, moving with lithe pantherish
grace round the desk to lean on its edge. His eyes
bored into her own, dissecting and assessing, as if
they possessed a licence to her soul.

'Your reason for instigating this—confrontation
intrigues me.' He indicated one of several deep-
seated armchairs with an indolent sweeping
gesture. 'Sit down.'

Determination, coupled with an inborn sense of
wariness, lifted her chin as a stoic denial left her
lips. 'I'd prefer to stand.'

The edge of his mouth formed a wry twist.
'Thereby assuming a position of near-flight?'

The first stirring of anger darkened her eyes to a
stormy grey. 'You're not making this very easy,'
she began, and he demanded with deceptive
softness,

'My dear Natalie, are you daring to suggest that I should?'

Resentment washed over her, leaving a tide of weariness. Personalities, however provocative, mustn't be permitted to intervene. 'My father is ill,' she stated flatly. 'A terminal disease that requires surgery and expensive treatment.'

There wasn't so much as a flicker of emotion apparent in those rugged features, and the ensuing silence seemed to reverberate around the room. Natalie was conscious of every breath she took, sure that the loud hammering of her heart must be audible.

Ryan Marshall's regard was swift and analytical, his eyes never leaving hers for a second. 'You have my sympathy.'

'But not your support,' Natalie stated with a tinge of bitterness, recognising no relenting in his manner.

'I wasn't aware that it had been requested,' he countered silkily, and she drew a deep calming breath.

'I didn't want to come here, much less appeal for help.' Her eyes regarded him steadily. 'You are my last resort, believe me.'

'How—flattering,' he acknowledged sardonically, and she met his gaze unwaveringly, seeing the inflexibility evident, and hated him afresh.

'Must I *beg*?'

'Would you?'

'Is that what you want?' she demanded bitterly.

There was a swift gleam in those tigerish eyes, and a cynical smile twisted the edge of his mouth. 'The inclination to see you on your knees is almost impossible to ignore.'

'My God, you're despicable!' Natalie asserted

with considerable force, and her eyes flashed as she rounded on him. 'I never imagined it possible to hate anyone as much as I hate you!'

'Have you finished?' he drawled imperturbably, although there was a warning softness evident that she refused to heed.

'Yes, *damn* you!' Anger set her features alive, her entire body seeming to reverberate with it. 'I was mad to come here—*insane* to think I might succeed.' She turned towards the door, filled with an incredible silent rage.

'Not so fast.' Somehow he was there before her, a towering formidable wall.

At such close proximity he was unsettling, the atmosphere between them charged with electrical force, and the knowledge that he still possessed the power to disturb her rose like bitter gall in her throat.

'You walked out of my life,' Ryan essayed softly—dangerously, and it took all Natalie's courage to stand quiescent beneath the force of his silent anger. 'Disappeared, seemingly without trace,' he continued ominously. 'No word— nothing, for three years.' One eyebrow lifted in silent mockery. 'And now you expect a simple "yes" or "no" answer to what amounts to a considerable sum of money?'

Put like that, it sounded ludicrous—something she had recognised from the start. Except that Andrea's subtle persuasion plus observance of her father's steady decline into ill-health, watching him deteriorate almost daily, had swept aside any misgivings.

'I should never have come,' she declared with resignation. Now, more than ever, she was convinced of it. With as much dignity as she could muster she made to move past him.

'There is a solution.'

Ryan's drawling tones brought her to a halt, and she slowly lifted her head.

'I hardly dare ask.' Her grey eyes were openly suspicious, and she schooled her composure to appear outwardly calm—an impossible task when her pulse-beat was accelerating crazily, and she lifted a hand to her throat in an attempt to hide its visible thudding.

'It's relatively simple,' he related quietly as he subjected her to a slow sweeping appraisal, his gaze fixed disturbingly on the soft outline of her mouth. 'We effect a reconciliation.'

Some inner voice screamed an agonised refusal, and for a wild moment she thought she had cried out that single monosyllabic negation. All vestige of colour left her features, leaving them pale and tense. It took every reserve of strength to remain civil, and the words came out stiffly—'I'm not that desperate!'

Ryan's eyes darkened until they resembled chips of topaz, and she felt an icy shiver scud down her spine at his dangerous compelling expression. Only a fool would dare cross a man such as he—yet she couldn't, *daren't*, agree to his proposition. Suddenly she was frighteningly aware of her own vulnerability—sure in the knowledge of his anger and the lengths to which his power could extend.

'No?'

That softly-voiced demand brought a momentary return of anger. *'No!'* Dear God, this was a thousand times worse than she had ever imagined possible.

'So emphatic,' Ryan mocked quietly, and without thought her hand flew to his face, the sound as it connected seeming unnecessarily loud in the stillness of the room.

The ensuing silence seemed interminable. A muscle tensed along his jaw, the only visible sign of his temper, and she wondered at her own temerity in providing provocation.

'I think I'd better leave,' she evinced in a strangled whisper, fear of subsequent retribution making escape imperative.

'If you don't,' Ryan bit out tersely, 'I'm liable to do something regrettable.'

How she managed to vacate the building without collapsing into an unenviable heap seemed a minor miracle. Inwardly she was shaking like a leaf, her composure torn to shreds at what had transpired, and in a trance she retraced her steps to the bus depot, purchased the necessary ticket and caught the next bus back to Brisbane where she was able to connect with another to Sydney.

Natalie reached the small country town of Casterton, located on the south-west Victorian border, utterly weary in both body and spirit. Having spent the past forty-eight hours travelling in cramped conditions and with insufficient rest, the thought of having to impart failure to her optimistic stepmother was almost the last straw. Andrea had been so positive an appeal to Ryan would succeed—the mere transition nothing less than a necessary formality.

A drawn-out sigh left Natalie's lips as she scanned the adjacent car park. It would have been nice to have been met, but the journey had been expensive enough without the additional expense of a trunk call notifying her arrival. A taxi was out, for she didn't possess sufficient money for the fare. In fact, she hadn't eaten since early that morning in an effort to conserve her funds. Calculating the evening's approaching dusk, she set out on foot, confident she would reach home before nightfall.

The wooden gate creaked as she passed through, and the lighted windows ahead were a welcoming sight as she mounted the steps.

Andrea's response to the doorbell was instantaneous. *'Natalie!'* Her perfectly-moulded features reflected an avid curiosity, demanding instant knowledge. 'How did you get on?'

Natalie had trouble summoning even a ghost of a smile. 'Don't I get offered a restoring cup of coffee first?' she countered with mild reproach. 'The last meal I had was breakfast.' She entered the small lounge and made for the kitchen. 'Is Dad asleep?'

'Likewise Michelle.' Andrea was right behind her, a faint murmur of apology on her lips. 'There's nothing left from dinner—I didn't know when to expect you.'

'I'll make do with a sandwich,' Natalie conceded, extracting a few slices of bread and selecting a filling from the refrigerator as Andrea set about making coffee.

'Well?'

Natalie met her stepmother's anxious gaze across the table and first took a bite from her sandwich, then a reviving gulp of steaming coffee.

There was no delaying the inevitable, and little point in embroidering unpleasant news. 'I'm sorry,' she said quietly, hating the disbelief that flickered across Andrea's face.

'You saw Ryan?'

'Yes, I saw him,' she agreed wearily.

'And he *refused*?'

'It wasn't a pleasant meeting.'

'But, dear God, he's your husband!' Andrea declared, appalled.

'We're separated, remember?' Natalie corrected wryly.

'You're still his legal wife,' her stepmother reminded her unnecessarily. 'If he knew about Michelle——'

'He doesn't,' Natalie interjected quickly, fixing the older woman with a warning look. 'And as long as I live, he'll never get the opportunity to lay claim to her.'

'You're a fool,' Andrea disclaimed vehemently. 'No one dismisses wealth in favour of poverty.'

Natalie felt weary beyond measure, her head ached, and she needed to catch up on some much-needed sleep. 'How has Dad been?' Her voice almost cracked with tiredness, and for a moment Andrea relented.

'Worse. I had to call the doctor twice while you were away. If he doesn't have surgery soon——' her voice trailed to a wretched halt, and Natalie saw the shine of unshed tears before the older woman managed to control them. 'For heaven's sake, go to bed—you look as if you're going to drop with fatigue. We'll talk tomorrow.'

The attic at the top of the narrow flight of stairs had been converted into a suite of rooms for Natalie more than seven years previously when her father had remarried. An only child, she had been sensitive to the relationship between her father and new stepmother, and enjoyed the feeling of independence in having her own private niche. It comprised a sitting-room, bedroom and adjoining bathroom, and she had been entirely responsible for the décor, and during the past three years she had never been more grateful for the retreat it offered.

Loath to disturb the sleeping child, Natalie didn't switch on the light, and she quietly gathered up a nightgown before moving through to the bathroom where she showered, then, refreshed, slipped beneath crisp cool sheets to drift within minutes into sweet oblivion.

Having been granted a week's leave of absence, the next few days were busy, for Natalie found a veritable pile of work awaiting her return. Her desk overflowed with it, necessitating minimum lunch breaks and often as much as an hour or two added on to her usual finishing time. Her employer was an elderly solicitor of indeterminate age, whose office she ran with single-handed efficiency. He had been so good about granting compassionate leave that she could hardly refuse to work doubly hard in an effort to bring her work up to date.

Consequently the time spent at home during Michelle's waking hours was minimal. There wasn't much opportunity to do more than look in on her father for more than ten minutes in the morning, and a further fifteen at night. If John Maclean had deduced a reason behind his daughter's sudden desire for a short vacation he gave no sign, and merely enquired if she had enjoyed herself. He appeared to tire more easily as each day passed, and watching him slowly fade filled her with a sense of helpless rage.

Saturday morning dawned bright and clear, promising sunshine in a contrary southern autumn climate, and after completing a few major chores Natalie strapped Michelle into the car-seat, then drove into town to pick up essential groceries.

It was a weekly ritual she enjoyed, although traversing each aisle with an increasingly mischievous two-year-old child had become something of an endurance test, requiring unlimited patience and a firm hand!

Having lived all her life in this small town—apart from a disastrous three months—Natalie knew every resident by name, and as was the pattern with country towns, knowledge of everyone's business was commonplace. Shopping in the town's centre was never a simple affair, as it inevitably involved several exchanges of conversation from the state of her father's health, Michelle's new tooth, a neighbour's rheumatism, to the state of the world in general.

Consequently it was almost one o'clock when she drove the small, rather careworn Mini into the garage and began unloading her purchases. Michelle had become fractious, the result of hunger and tiredness, and it took almost an hour before order was restored and blissful peace reigned as the little girl slept.

'Coffee, or a cool drink?'

'Coffee,' Natalie answered without hesitation, giving a faint smile as she regarded her stepmother across the kitchen table. 'I need reviving.'

'I'll have one, too,' Andrea agreed, standing to her feet. 'I'll make it. You look tired.'

'I didn't think it showed that much,' she murmured with self-mockery. They had just finished a light lunch, and suddenly noticing her father's tray wasn't resting on the servery, Natalie moved away from the table with the intention of retrieving it.

'John isn't here,' Andrea said quickly. 'He's been taken for a drive.'

Natalie stopped in her tracks, surprise uppermost. 'Is that wise? He was in a great deal of pain this morning.'

The kettle whistled and Andrea poured boiling

water over instant coffee, then placed the cups on the table.

'Sit down, Natalie.'

Something in her stepmother's tone brought a slight frown, and Natalie gave her a sharp look. 'What's the matter?' Her eyes narrowed, then widened with sudden disbelieving comprehension. 'You didn't——'

'Contact Ryan?' her stepmother completed defensively. 'Yes. Two days ago.'

'You had no right!' The words tumbled from Natalie's lips in a rush of anger, and she saw the older woman's mouth tighten into a determined line.

'I consider I had ever right,' Andrea insisted, and sank down into a chair, her fingers shaking as she extracted a cigarette from its packet and lit it, then she exhaled a stream of smoke as if the nicotine alone could supply a measure of courage. Her eyes beseeched Natalie to understand. 'Can't you see I had no choice?'

'You could have told me first!' Natalie cried indignantly, only to hear her stepmother's voice say quietly,

'So that you could run away—again? Eventually you'll run out of places to hide. Then what?' she queried a trifle grimly. 'Ryan has a right to know of Michelle's existence,' she added, her eyes glittering with indignation.

'*Rights!*' Natalie demanded in utter condemnation. 'What about *my* rights? Don't they deserve some consideration?'

Andrea released an angry puff of smoke and threw her stepdaughter an angry glare. 'We've sheltered you for three years, Natalie—fabricated lies concerning your whereabouts during the initial enquiries Ryan made after you'd left him.' Her eyes softened slightly, silently pleading. 'You've had every support we could offer. Now I have to think of your father.'

'At my expense,' Natalie declared bitterly, then could have bitten her tongue. 'I'm sorry,' she apologised, instantly contrite. 'That was a selfish thing to say.'

A long-drawn-out sigh left the older woman's lips. 'Ryan rang this morning while you were out, confirming arrangements he had made for your father. Late this morning an ambulance transported John to the nearest airport, where he'll be flown to Sydney and admitted to hospital. By this evening he'll be in the care of one of the finest medical teams in the country.'

Natalie felt as if a hand was tightly squeezing her heart. 'You'll follow Dad, of course,' she said matter-of-factly.

'I fly out tomorrow,' Andrea revealed slowly. 'I have a sister in one of the inner city suburbs with whom I can stay.'

'How will you get on for money?' It was a question Natalie had to ask, even though she already knew the answer.

For an instant her stepmother wavered, then defended with hardly a trace of guilt, 'Ryan has advanced sufficient funds to release me of any worry.'

Natalie felt her stomach contract, and her whole body began to ache with an inexplicable pain. 'In return, he gets Michelle,' she pronounced through white lips.

'Don't be ridiculous,' Andrea protested. 'He can't abduct her.'

Natalie directed the older woman a levelling glance. 'Can't he?' Her voice was totally sceptical. 'Ryan Marshall is a law unto himself!'

'He struck me as a fair-minded man,' Andrea defended, and Natalie gave a derisive laugh.

'He's hard, and totally without any scruples,' she declared.

'Nonsense. I don't believe——'

'Michelle is *mine*, and nobody, not even Ryan, is going to take her away from me.' Natalie stood blindly to her feet. 'I'm going to pack, and leave—*now*.' Plans raced willy-nilly through her brain. 'The Mini—you won't need it for the next few months——'

The insistent peal of the doorbell provided an interruption, sounding unnecessarily loud to her tautly stretched nerves, and she swung back towards Andrea, her eyes stark with fear.

'You're too late.' There was an element of regret in the older woman's voice, a sense of concern, and her eyes clouded as Natalie said bitterly,

'Thanks, Andrea. Your timing is lousy!'

'Won't you at least let him in?' Andrea entreated.

'The hell I will!' she refused vehemently. 'It's your house, *you* let him in. I'm going upstairs.' She had almost left the room when the doorbell pealed a further summons, and Andrea stood to her feet, smoothed her hair, then attempted to ease some of the tension from her features.

'Michelle's asleep,' she warned quietly, and Natalie hardly paused as she crossed the hall and ascended the stairs.

'With the battle about to be fought,' she shot pitilessly, 'I imagine she'll wake, regardless!'

On reaching her suite of rooms she quietly closed the door and leaned against it, momentarily shutting her eyes in an attempt to dispel the blind panic that drained her face of any vestige of colour.

Slowly she opened her eyes and for a moment their expression was blank, then she stirred herself sufficiently to walk into the bedroom where her daughter lay sleeping in a white-painted bed beneath the window.

A fierce protectiveness filled her breast as she gazed down at the child, cherubic in sleep. Light wispy blonde hair and pale creamy skin, she was Natalie in miniature—except for a pair of knowing gold-hazel eyes that, when open, were entirely Ryan's.

A short double knock on the outer door jolted her into awareness, and with a deep steadying breath Natalie slowly moved from the bedroom to the cheerfully-furnished sitting-room.

Just as she reached the door it swung open, and Natalie felt a frisson of fear slither down her spine at the sight of the man filling its aperture. Of its own volition her chin lifted in silent defiance, and for one unguarded second she glimpsed naked savagery in his expression before it was successfully masked.

Silence rebounded around the room until it became unbearable, and she almost choked attempting to swallow the lump that rose unbidden to her throat.

CHAPTER TWO

'SHALL we dispense with any pleasantries, and go straight into battle?' Natalie heard her voice, shaky with anger, and wondered dispassionately if it belonged to someone else. There was a strange feeling of unreality about the scene. Ryan—*here*. Something she had had recurring nightmares about during the past few years, waking in a cold sweat that he had managed to elicit information leading to her whereabouts—worse, discovered the wild passion they had once shared had borne fruit in the form of a child. Hers, but indisputably *his*.

A muscle tensed along his powerful jaw, adding emphasis to a profile that was arresting.

'I didn't come here to fight,' Ryan declared with clipped cynicism, and she uttered a disbelieving laugh.

'You surprise me!'

'Aren't you going to ask me in?' he countered, and with an exaggerated gesture she stood to one side.

'By all means, let's be civil about the whole thing.'

'Andrea saw fit to contact me,' Ryan declared with an edge of mockery as he moved to the centre of the room, and Natalie met his hard gaze with a touch of defiance.

'So I've just been informed.' Her grey eyes resembled the bleakness of a storm-tossed sea. 'My father gets taken care of—one can only presume in the best of private hospitals. Andrea has all burden of debt lifted from her shoulders.'

Bitterness clouded her features, intermingled with angry rejection. 'I can understand Andrea's methods, but I won't pretend to condone them.'

For a moment Ryan's eyes gleamed with anger, and when he spoke his voice was dangerously soft. 'How do you think I reacted on discovering I have a child?'

Sparks flew from her eyes as she threw wildly, 'If it had been left to me, you'd never have known of her existence!'

'I could strangle you with my bare hands,' Ryan intimated mercilessly, and for a few heartstopping seconds she experienced genuine fear. He looked capable of anything, his superior strength reducing her to a state of defenceless impotence.

'Assault is a punishable offence,' Natalie declared warily.

It seemed an age before he spoke, and when he did his voice was devoid of any emotion. 'I want my daughter.'

Anger erupted from her throat like lava from an active volcano. 'You can't have her!' Her eyes flashed with bitter enmity as she lashed, 'I'll fight you in every court in the country!'

'Any judge would award me custody,' Ryan declared silkily, 'on the grounds that my ability to provide for her well-being is far superior to yours.'

Each word hammered home with chilling finality, and Natalie's voice rasped with disbelieving incredulity. 'I won't let you take her,' she whispered. 'You'll hand her over to a highly competent nanny, then bundle her off to boarding school the minute she becomes eligible.' The words had difficulty getting past the lump in her throat, and her body seemed racked with pain. 'What kind of monster are you?'

'A very human one,' he answered quietly, his eyes holding hers unwaveringly. 'I want you back.'

She looked at him, aghast. 'You can't be serious?'

'Utterly.'

'What is this—*revenge*?'

'Call it whatever you like.'

'And if I refuse?'

'You won't.' His smile was singularly humourless. 'Michelle is my trump card.'

'You—bastard,' Natalie whispered futilely.

'Such language!' Ryan chastised mockingly, and Natalie rounded on him in utter fury.

'Go to hell!'

'Be careful I don't take you with me,' he taunted softly.

'Words fail to express how much I hate you!'

'My heart bleeds,' he drawled sardonically, his lips moving to form a cynical smile. 'Our—er—reconciliation won't be without its compensations.'

'I don't give a damn for any so-called compensations!'

His expression hardened measurably. 'We fly out tomorrow, Natalie,' he declared with marked inflexibility. 'Andrea will accompany us as far as Sydney. I suggest you begin packing.'

'You're joking!' she exclaimed, horrified as her brain began whirling at the implications such a transition involved.

'Not in the least,' Ryan denied wryly, regarding her through narrowed eyes.

'The house can't be left unattended——'

'It's all been arranged, Natalie,' he told her cynically, and she gave a bitter laugh.

'Of course—forgive me. I'm merely a pawn in this diabolical charade.'

'Hardly a charade,' he reminded her sardonically, and she forced herself to speak with a semblance of civility.

'Having acquainted me of the details, will you please leave?'

One eyebrow slanted with mocking cynicism. 'This room, or the house?'

'*Both!*'

'Andrea is very hospitable,' Ryan disclosed dispassionately. 'She offered me a bed for the night.'

'Not *mine*,' Natalie declared vehemently, and his lips twisted into a faint smile.

'So adamant, my darling wife. I vividly recall a time when you leapt at the chance.'

'I was a besotted fool,' she muttered in an unsteady voice, fixing her gaze on a spot to the left of his shoulder.

'Three years, Natalie,' he mused cynically. 'Dare I hope you've grown up?'

Resentment welled up inside her, sharpening her tongue. 'If by growing up you mean I might condone a mistress or two, or more, then you're sadly mistaken!'

Ryan's expression became keenly alert. 'What the hell are you talking about?'

'Simone Vesey.' Natalie revealed with succinct sarcasm, and an eyebrow slanted in a gesture of mockery.

'What do you want? A blow-by-blow account of every woman I've bedded since puberty?'

'My word!' she breathed unevenly. 'You mean, you remember them *all*?'

The air crackled with latent animosity, a reminder of his temper evident in the chilling glint from his topaz eyes, and she unconsciously held her breath, waiting for an inevitable verbal onslaught.

'Is there anything to be gained in pursuing this conversation?' he demanded dryly, and she released a long-drawn-out sigh.

'I admire your adroitness in escaping the issue.'

'I wasn't aware Simone Vesey *was* an issue.'

'Oh really, Ryan,' Natalie mocked with derision, 'I didn't come down with the last shower of rain!'

'I could slap you, do you know that?' he declared silkily after a measurable silence.

'My goodness, is that a threat?' she countered sweetly, and saw his eyes darken ominously.

'Don't tempt me,' he began hardily. 'I have a thin rein on my temper as it is.'

'Why?' she demanded huskily. 'Is your ego dampened to discover the child you fathered is female, rather than a coveted son?'

For a moment Natalie thought he would explode, and she wondered at her own temerity in rousing his anger. The result wasn't an enviable quality, and she retained too vivid a memory of past retributions to want to incur any repeat.

'What you're doing amounts to coercion,' she proffered shakily, and he arched a sardonic eyebrow.

'Do you want to change your mind?'

With an unconscious movement she lifted a hand and smoothed back a stray tendril of hair behind her ear. There was no defiance in her manner, just a kind of desperate curiosity. 'What would you do if I did?'

'Take Michelle.' There was a terrible finality in those words that didn't bear thinking about.

'You're despicable,' Natalie whispered, appalled. 'I'm her mother!'

'I'm also her father.'

The words tumbled forth with choked incoherency. 'I'll never forgive you for this!'

His slow smile was a mere facsimile. 'My heart bleeds.'

He was nothing less than a callous *brute,* and she was about to tell him so when a thin piercing cry erupted from the adjoining room, rapidly ascending to a fractious wail, and without a word Natalie turned in escape to tend to her daughter's needs.

Michelle was sitting up in bed, her lips puckered in distress, two large tears slowly wending their way down her childish cheeks. The instant she caught sight of Natalie her small arms reached out and her face became wreathed in a full-dimpled smile.

'Had a nice nap, darling?' Natalie asked, crossing to take the little girl into her arms. Her lips moved down to nuzzle the sweet crease at Michelle's neck. No one, not even Ryan, was going to deprive her of the most important possession in her life.

With easy adeptness Natalie changed the little tot into her clothes, then she swung her into her arms for a customary cuddle. Michelle responded by chuckling with delight.

'May I?'

Natalie hadn't heard a sound, nothing to indicate that Ryan had followed her into the bedroom, and she turned slowly, her arms shielding her daughter as if from some predatory aggressor.

His eyes met hers unwaveringly, silently demanding she comply, and her chin lifted of its own volition. Her hold on Michelle instinctively tightened as she glimpsed his savage anger.

Heaven knew what would have happened next if Michelle, fascinated by the sight of a strange man, hadn't suddenly decided to proffer Ryan a singularly sweet smile.

'Hello there,' he greeted her quietly, his lips widening into a slow lopsided smile, and immediately was rewarded with a gurgling chuckle.

'I usually take her downstairs for a glass of milk and a cereal biscuit,' Natalie put in stiffly.

'Then I suggest you let me do so. Andrea can supply the sustenance while I become better acquainted with my daughter.'

'While I do—what?'

The smile was still evident, but his eyes were dark golden chips. 'Pack,' he instructed succinctly, daring her to defy him as he moved and took Michelle from her arms.

The door opened, then closed quietly behind him, and it was with a supreme effort that Natalie managed to control the urge to throw something in his wake! She would have taken much satisfaction in the action—no matter how futile!

Impotent rage clouded her gaze as she retrieved a suitcase from the wardrobe, and flinging it on to the bed she threw clothes into it with no compunction for their neatness. Michelle's favourite toys were placed into a large overnight bag, then she did a quick mental check that no necessities had been overlooked.

At the lower edge of the narrow staircase Natalie paused and drew a deep steadying breath before moving towards the lounge. Her eyes were suspiciously bright as she met Andrea's quick darting gaze, and the tight little smile she summoned forth didn't fool anyone.

Ryan was seated comfortably in an armchair with Michelle positioned on one powerful thigh, the little girl appearing totally enchanted with the new man in her life as she busily attempted to unbutton his shirt.

Learning at an early age, Natalie thought silently, and caught the faint cynicism in his gleaming eyes. Damn him—he had always been adept at reading her mind!

'How about a drink?' Andrea suggested brightly.

'Ryan? Whisky, if I remember correctly. And Natalie, a light sherry?'

Oh, for the sanity of preserving the conventions, Natalie mocked silently as she accepted the glass of amber liquid.

'I've organised dinner,' Andrea prattled, aware that the tension within the room could be sliced with a proverbial knife. 'You will dine with us, Ryan?'

He inclined his head in silent acquiescence. 'Thank you.'

Natalie darted him a glance that held thinly-veiled venom, and was met with an expression of musing mockery. Damn him! He seemed bent on deliberately making things as awkward for her as possible! Her mood verged on dangerous anti-pathy, and the alcohol gave her the impetus to query, 'Perhaps one of you would care to enlighten me as to the extent of the information Dad has been given regarding the sudden availability of funds?' Her eyes burned with ill-concealed fury as she evinced with deliberate sarcasm, 'After all, our stories should match, don't you think?'

Andrea glanced nervously at Ryan, who asserted with silky smoothness,

'John has been told the truth.' He paused deliberately, then continued blandly, 'Your recent—holiday was instrument in achieving a reconciliation. Naturally, upon learning of my father-in-law's illness, I insisted on assuming responsibility for any medical expenses.'

'*Naturally*,' Natalie echoed dryly. She could only admire their conspiracy. It had all been carefully planned, and doubtless Andrea felt justified in sparing John any unpleasantness. It was the one thing that was commendable in the entire misadventure!

'Sarcasm doesn't suit you,' Ryan slanted

imperturbably, and she gave a wry laugh, emptying the contents of her glass before crossing to the cabinet to refill it from the decanter.

'What do you expect? Polite conversation?'

Andrea shifted slightly on her chair, attempting to deal with an awkward situation as best she knew how. 'We've had a very mild summer,' she began, directing her attention to Ryan. 'How has the weather been on the Coast?'

'Oh, by all means,' Natalie intervened facetiously, 'let's discuss the weather.'

'Contrary,' Ryan answered, blandly ignoring his wife. 'With the highest rainfall recorded in more than a decade.'

'Interesting how the seasons appear to have changed over the years,' Andrea commented, as if the topic consumed a vital interest, and Natalie felt stifled by the banality of the situation.

'If you'll excuse me,' she said abruptly, 'I'll leave the two of you to discuss the state of the world.' She glanced towards Andrea. 'I'll unpeg the washing from the line, and prepare Michelle's vegetables.' Offering a bright smile, she barely skimmed Ryan with her gaze, hating the ease with which Michelle had accepted him. 'I'm sure the two of you can manage quite well without me.'

Dinner was not the dreaded event Natalie had imagined it might be, for with sophisticated adroitness Ryan managed to maintain a conversational flow, despite her often monosyllabic response. It didn't seem to bother him a whit whether she participated or not.

At the end of the meal, Natalie rose to her feet with alacrity. 'I'll attend to the dishes.' She collected plates and began stacking them, refusing to meet those dark musing eyes across the table.

'Irish coffee, Ryan?' Andrea suggested, appearing relaxed and at ease. 'A nice finishing touch, don't you agree?'

'I'll set the coffee on to perk.' Natalie escaped into the kitchen with a sense of relief, despite the seemingly mountainous pile of saucepans, crockery and cutlery that needed to be washed. Andrea had really surpassed herself with dinner, applying all her culinary skills and succeeding beautifully—although dealing with the aftermath took considerable time before order was restored.

With the coffee made, its tantalising aroma teased the tastebuds as Natalie placed three mugs on to a tray and carried it into the lounge, whereupon Andrea looked up with a trace of guilt.

'I should have given you some help.'

'Nonsense,' Natalie dismissed. 'You couldn't neglect our guest.'

'Good heavens,' the older woman exclaimed in mild amazement, 'Ryan is more than a mere guest?'

Natalie chose silence, deliberately avoiding his gaze as he took a mug from the proffered tray, then seating herself in a single armchair on the opposite side of the room she pondered just how soon she could decently retire without making her exit too glaringly obvious.

'Will it be convenient if we leave around seven in the morning?'

She glanced up at the sound of that drawling voice, centring her attention somewhere in the vicinity of his left ear. 'I'm surprised you bother to ask.' A tinge of cynicism entered her voice. 'I imagined you'd have the arrangements made, without referring to me as to their suitability.'

'You didn't answer the question.'

Her smoky grey eyes shifted to meet his. 'How are we travelling?' she asked levelly, and felt her heart give a sudden lurch as Andrea stood to her feet, for all the world intent on declaring her need for an early night.

'You will excuse me, won't you?' Andrea's smile encompassed them both. 'I'll leave you to settle the finer details. Goodnight.'

Don't go! Natalie wanted to scream. For God's sake, don't leave me alone with him! But it was too late, for the older woman was already at the door, her departing smile a stark reminder of Natalie's vulnerability.

Ryan regarded her steadily, his expression enigmatic. He appeared totally at ease, and it was all she could do not to turn and flee.

After what seemed an interminable silence, he informed her in a lazy drawl. 'A chartered Lear jet will take us to Sydney. After ensuring that Andrea is safely met by her sister, we'll fly on to Coolangatta.'

'Where your car is waiting,' she concluded, and glimpsed his wry smile.

'Yes.'

Standing to her feet, Natalie collected the mugs and the tray with the intention of taking them through to the kitchen.

'In such a hurry to escape my company?' His mocking drawl brought forth a surge of latent anger.

'It's been a very wearying day,' she retorted with asperity, spearing him with a stormy glance. 'Tomorrow won't be any better, travelling from dawn to sunset. I intend getting a full night's sleep.'

Ryan's mouth twisted into a sardonic smile. 'Your last alone, Natalie. Enjoy it.'

For a heartstopping moment she was tempted to throw the tray and its contents at his hateful head, then sanity prevailed. Without bothering to look at him, she walked from the room, and in the kitchen she rinsed the mugs and put them to drain, then replaced the tray.

There was no means by which to reach the stairs without going through the lounge, and she studiously avoided glancing at Ryan as she moved towards the hall.

'Andrea failed to indicate where I'm to sleep.' His voice reached her just as she was about to open the door, and she turned to see the lazy mockery evident in his expression.

'The guest room is to the right of the stairs,' Natalie told him bleakly. 'I'll check that the bed has been made up.'

The fact that it hadn't filled her with silent rage. Damn Andrea for placing her in such an invidious position! It was all Natalie could do not to fling the necessary sheets and blankets on to the bed and instruct Ryan to make it up himself.

The chore was completed in a matter of minutes, and her face was a stony mask as she attempted to move past him.

The elusive woodsy tang of his aftershave teased her nostrils as she drew close. Every last nerve-end tingled into awareness, making her shockingly aware of him, and there was no willpower in the world able to halt the faint tinge of pink that crept over her cheeks. Three years—more than a thousand *nights*, hadn't dimmed the electrifying hunger, the *need*, that she had deliberately buried deep inside herself.

Dear God, what was the matter with her! How could she respond like this when she hated him— *hated*, with every fibre in her body! It was madness, some temporary form of insanity. It *had* to be!

A slight movement alerted her attention, and with a sense of terrible fascination she watched as Ryan lifted a hand and idly traced the outline of her lips.

'Are you staying?'

The soft drawl acted like a douche of cold water, and she wrenched away, filled with sickening despair. 'No—*no*!'

She reached the safety of her room, hardly aware of having ascended the stairs, and leaned against the closed door, her breathing as heavy and spasmodic as if she had just run a mile.

It was a long time before she roused herself sufficiently to move towards her bedroom, where she slowly and mechanically went through the motions of preparing for bed.

Slipping between the sheets, she buried her head into the pillow with an audible groan as painful memories came flooding back in a sequence of hauntingly vivid events, making sleep impossible.

CHAPTER THREE

It had begun with a carefree holiday Natalie shared with two girl friends, each taking three weeks' annual leave, and intent on enjoying as much fun and sun as the famed Queensland coastal resort of Surfer's Paradise claimed to provide.

On the fourth evening, *Thursday*—dear God, she could even remember the day, the *hour*—they had elected to visit a disco, where during the course of the evening she had been unable to deter the amorous clutches of her partner and had signalled her friends that she intended to leave.

Thinking nothing of walking the two blocks to the hotel, she had viewed the four young revellers ahead with scant regard until they surrounded her, jostling and jeering as they halted her progress. At first she had smiled and stepped aside, then when they refused to let her pass she unloosed a few pithy words with little effect, and just as things began to get out of hand a tall lean stranger appeared on the scene, and in a matter of seconds the youths were gone.

'Thank you,' Natalie proffered gratefully, turning to her rescuer with a slight smile. 'That was fast becoming a sticky situation.'

'You're a visitor to the Coast?'

It was more a statement than a query, and she gave a light chuckle. 'Is it that obvious?' In the dimly-lit side-street all she could determine was a tall well-built frame.

'It isn't wise to walk alone here at night,' her

rescuer drawled. 'If you must, choose one of the main streets where there are plenty of people.'

'I didn't think,' Natalie found herself saying with total honesty. 'The hotel is only a short distance away, and the Esplanade seemed the quickest route.'

'If you don't want a recurrence of that nasty episode, I suggest you allow me to drive you back to your hotel.'

'And jump from the frying pan straight into the fire?' she retorted with a faint laugh. 'Thanks—but no, thanks.'

'Such independence!' he mocked quizzically, and she responded cautiously,

'Having just delivered a warning on "stranger-danger", you contradict yourself by suggesting I get into your car.'

He was walking beside her, within touching distance, and he laughed—a deep throaty chuckle that made her turn and look at him.

The illumination from a nearby street light threw his features sharply into focus, outlining a broad-chiselled profile with an arresting quality that sent shock-waves slithering down the length of her spine.

'So—no car,' he mocked, and his firm sensuously-moulded mouth widened into a smile. 'By your own admittance, the hotel isn't far. We'll walk.'

Natalie gave a faint shrug. 'It really isn't necessary.'

'Call it my good deed for the day.'

She wrinkled her nose at him, and her eyes danced with ill-concealed humour. 'You don't look the Boy Scout type.'

His answering smile did strange things to her equilibrium. 'Just what *do* I look like?'

Her head tilted to one side as she regarded him. 'Hmm—sophisticated,' she proffered pensively. 'Successful, I'd say. You have that certain air. And popular with the fairer sex.'

'Not trustworthy? Reliable?'

Natalie laughed, and it was a sweet melodic sound, without pretention. 'I'd have to know you a lot better before I'd dare to pass comment on those qualities.'

'Have dinner with me tomorrow night.' It wasn't a question, it was a statement—expecting acceptance.

'I'm holidaying with two friends,' she refused politely.

'Who can surely spare you for one night?'

'No—thank you. I don't know you—anything about you,' she explained carefully. They had almost reached the end of the second block, and her hotel lay just across the street, its entrance ablaze with light.

'Do you have a name?'

She looked at him squarely, sensing a dangerous, compelling quality—an inherent determination to conquer any obstacle that stood in his way. Accepting a date with him would be akin to diving off a jetty into unknown depths in the dark of night! 'I don't think my name is important,' she said quietly. 'Thank you for providing an escort. Goodnight.'

Not waiting for his response, she stepped from the pavement and crossed to the hotel, entering its portals and summoning the elevator without so much as a backward glance.

During the following few days the three girls alternately shopped and sunbathed, electing on Saturday night to take in a much-advertised floorshow held at an international hotel.

It was halfway through the evening during an intermission that Natalie experienced a strange prickling sensation at the base of her nape, and turning slowly to discover the cause she came face to face with none other than her tall dynamic rescuer. Her smile was little more than a polite acknowledgment. of his presence before she turned back to converse with her friends.

What happened next was unexpected, but afterwards she could only view the encounter with musing resignation.

'May I offer to get you a drink?' The deep drawling voice from close behind simultaneously accompanied his light touch at her elbow, and even before she turned she could see the effect his presence was having on both her friends.

Susan, the more vivacious of the three, recognising an opportunity too good to let slip through her fingers immediately rose to the occasion and accepted with gracious alacrity.

The inevitable introductions were effected, and it seemed a refusal to join his table was unavoidable—impossible, when Susan had already accepted on their behalf!

Ryan Marshall proved himself to be an attentive host, and without being aware of it Natalie found she had been subtly included in an invitation to his home the following evening.

After the show he insisted on driving the three girls back to their hotel, and on parting instructed that they be ready at seven the next evening.

'We'll get a taxi,' Natalie said a trifle desperately, only to be foiled in the attempt by his insistence that he would call for them.

Choosing what to wear and the ensuing preparations for the evening ahead seemed to take most of the day, although despite all opposition

Natalie elected to wear a simply-cut dress in aquamarine silk, its bodice gathered at the waist, creating a blouson effect, the skirt falling a few inches below her knees. The colour highlighted the fairness of her hair and gave her lightly tanned skin an added glow. High-heeled strappy sandals and a matching white clutch purse were a perfect complement, and although she applied make-up with care, she chose an understated look, using a minimum of eyeshadow and mascara, and merely smoothed a shiny gloss over her lips.

She settled into the front seat of the luxurious vehicle with a sense of trepidation. Ryan Marshall was no ordinary man. The car he drove was an expensive foreign model, and it seemed her worst fears were confirmed when he took the turn-off leading to an exclusive inner island suburb.

Cronin Island was the smallest and perhaps the most prestigious of the island developments, for Surfer's Paradise was a long coastal strip whose inner islands lay along the meandering Nerang River and were linked to the mainland by several bridges. Developers had had the foresight to gauge the Coast's potential, and over the years had developed the small islands into canal estates, continuing canal development on to the mainland fringes. The result was unique, providing highly sought-after real estate. No visit to the tourist mecca was complete without taking a cruise along the canal waterways, receiving colourful commentary on the history of the canal development, and an opportunity to view some of the more famous millionaire residences.

The evening possessed an unreal quality from the moment Ryan swept the car between high electronically-controlled wrought-iron gates and brought it to a halt in the forecourt of what could only be described as a mansion. Guests began arriving shortly after eight, and during the ensuing hours Natalie was supremely conscious of his every glance, the slight almost secretive smile he gave her whenever their eyes seemed to meet—which was often. Some form of elusive magic was pulling them together, and she appeared powerless to stop it. Common sense screamed for her to run as fast and as far as she could. Ryan Marshall, whatever—*whoever* he was, was a thousand light years apart from the life she led, and to become involved with him in any way was asking for heartache.

It was Natalie's insistence that resulted in the three girls getting a taxi back to the hotel. Her polite refusal to have Ryan drive them drew forth a faint teasing smile, and when the taxi drew up outside the gates he leant out a hand and idly brushed his fingers down her cheek in a strangely gentle gesture.

'Goodnight, Natalie.' His voice was a soft seductive drawl, and despite the warm evening air, she shivered.

At nine the following morning he phoned with an invitation to dinner that evening. Politely but firmly, she refused, and put down the receiver.

When the girls returned from the beach that afternoon there was a cellophane-wrapped florist's box containing one single red rose, and a card indicating that he would call at six-thirty.

'No,' Natalie insisted, when she was alternately pleaded with and berated by her friends.

'For heaven's sake—he's *gorgeous*!' Susan wailed in despair. 'What have you got to lose?'

My sanity—among other things! she wanted to scream. Instead she said calmly, 'I'm not going out with him.'

'You mean you'll stay here and tell him so when he arrives?'

'No.' She wasn't that brave! 'I'll leave a message at the desk.' She wrinkled her nose at them, inveigling, 'How about dinner at the Pizza Hut, or McDonald's—followed by a movie?'

They complied, albeit reluctantly, returning to the hotel after eleven, and the next morning there was a further floral tribute—this time the message read, 'I'm serious. Seven this evening. Ryan'. Half an hour later the phone rang.

'It's for you,' Susan announced, holding the receiver out towards Natalie, who shook her head, mouthing a silent message relaying her absence from the apartment.

Ten minutes later there was a knock at the door, and Natalie flew into the bedroom. 'If it's who I think it is——' she paused, her eyes wide as a gamut of emotions darkened their depths, 'I'm down at the beach—or in the pool—anywhere,' she finished blindly.

It didn't do any good. Three minutes later the door opened, and Ryan was in the room, his lengthy frame leaning with indolent ease against the wall.

'You can't come in—this is a bedroom,' Natalie almost stammered, her eyes wide with consternation as she gazed at him.

'Correction,' he drawled. 'It's a room in which there are two beds—somewhere you've escaped in order to avoid me. Why?'

'Can't you accept that I won't go out with you?' she countered, her grey eyes serious.

'You don't wear a ring proclaiming any man's right of possession,' Ryan declared quietly. 'Is it possible you're afraid of me?'

He was too perceptive by far! 'Yes,' she

admitted starkly. Worse, afraid of myself, she added silently.

His voice was deep and wholly serious. 'I'd like the opportunity to get to know you.'

A choking, faintly scornful laugh left her lips. 'Don't you mean "get me into bed"?'

Dark golden eyes flared briefly with anger, then his mouth twisted into a wry smile. 'That, too.'

Natalie had difficulty in swallowing. 'I don't go in for transient relationships,' she responded steadily, and his eyebrow slanted in quizzical appraisal.

'Meaning that I do?'

'Look,' she began desperately, 'you're probably a very nice man. In fact, you look——' she searched for an appropriate word, and failed. 'Susan would go out with you in a flash,' she rushed, throwing her hands out in a gesture of despair. 'Why *me*?'

'Dinner tonight,' Ryan insisted softly. 'If you don't agree, I'll bundle you into the car *now*.'

She felt her eyes widen into large pools of incredulity. 'You can't do that!'

'Can't I?' he mocked lightly, and she made one last attempt.

'What about your job—you must work at something!'

'I've decided to delegate responsibility today.' He moved from the door and advanced slowly towards her. 'We're going out. No,' he paused, and placed a finger to her lips, 'no arguments.'

'My friends——'

'If having them along means I get *you*, by all means ask them.'

It was an enjoyable day, as Ryan drove to out-of-the-way spots, places the tourist buses rarely frequented, and if he intended that the time spent in his company might melt her resistance, he succeeded.

The restaurant was small and secluded, eliciting the patronage of the socially élite, and it wasn't until Natalie had sipped a full glass of wine that she began to relax a little.

'Tell me about yourself.'

She glanced at the man opposite and proffered a slight smile. 'Age, rank and serial number?' she quipped lightly. 'Really, I'm very uninteresting. From an ordinary middle-class family, comprising father, stepmother—no brothers or sisters. I've lived all my life in a small country town near the south-west border of Victoria. I'm nineteen years of age, and I work for an elderly solicitor.' The wine was giving her courage—perhaps she should have some more! 'Your turn.'

'Thirty-two, a family well scattered in several different countries throughout the world. Development and construction is my business.'

Her eyes sparkled with hidden laughter. 'Very concisely compiled. You must be very successful,' she added, and met his thoughtful gaze.

'Yes. Does it bother you?'

'Wealth can't buy health or happiness,' she said slowly.

'It helps,' he assured her with mocking cynicism.

'I imagine it does,' Natalie agreed seriously. 'Although I'd hate to be unsure whether my friends liked me for myself, or merely for the material possessions my wealth could provide.'

His eyes narrowed thoughtfully. 'You're too clever by far—do you know that?'

Very carefully she lifted her glass and took a tentative sip. 'This is an excellent wine.'

A slow smile teased the edges of his mouth, and he raised his glass in a silent mocking toast.

The food surpassed anything she had ever tasted, and as the evening progressed she began to view its end with mixed emotions. Sure that she needed all her faculties alert and not undermined by alcohol, she refused to have her glass refilled. It didn't elude her that Ryan was well aware of the reason why, and what was more, found the fact amusing.

In the car she was silent, unable to think of a thing to say that wouldn't come out as inane or inconsequential. It took all of four minutes to reach the hotel, yet each one seemed like an hour, and when Ryan brought the vehicle to a halt she sat still, longing to flee from his presence yet not quite able to summon the courage to do so.

'Is it all men who have this effect—or just me?'

Natalie endeavoured to evade the issue. 'Thank you for a pleasant evening.' She reached for the door clasp, only to be forestalled.

'You're trembling—why?' he demanded softly. 'I haven't the slightest intention of harming so much as a hair on your beautiful head.'

'It's late,' she ventured a trifle desperately, and he smiled. Without a word he leaned an arm along the back of her seat and bent towards her. His warm breath fanned her cheek, then his lips touched an earlobe before trailing slowly down the edge of her jaw to the corner of her mouth.

It was a gentle caress, provocative and faintly teasing, momentary, and leaving her with a strange bereft feeling as he reached for the clasp to unlatch her door.

'Goodnight, Natalie.' His voice bore a trace of mockery, and she slipped from the car, her reciprocal murmur lost in the sound of the soft clunk as the door closed behind her.

In a daze she walked to the entrance and

inserted her key into the security lock, and when the doors slid shut behind her she turned and caught a glimpse of gleaming paintwork as the racy Ferrari slipped out on to the road.

For some unknown reason she wanted to cry. He had made no mention of ringing, nor had he suggested another date. She tried to tell herself she didn't care, but how else could she explain the strange ache deep inside her?

With the dawn came reason and a resolve to forget the compelling Ryan Marshall. Natalie was evasive when begged to relate every detail of the previous evening, and dispelled the inclination to stay close to the phone in case it rang, choosing instead to spend the day at the beach. There were no messages at reception on their return, and with a feeling of desperation she suggested they eat out, attend a nightclub—anything, in an attempt to be caught up in noise and laughter so that her attention was diverted away from the man who had begun to fill her thoughts to such a degree that it was vaguely frightening.

The next morning she was dragged from sleep by the sound of the phone ringing, and she flew to answer it, unsuspecting in a state of half-wakefulness as to who might be calling at such an early hour.

'Natalie?'

She slumped against the wall, unable to find her voice for a few seconds, and Ryan's deep drawl held amusement.

'Did I get you out of bed?'

Hastily she consulted her watch. 'It's seven o'clock.'

'And you're standing there in a demure cotton shift with your hair all tousled,' he mused, and she could sense the laughter in his voice.

'I have no intention of telling you anything about my sleeping attire,' she declared unsteadily, and heard a deep-throated chuckle in response.

'I'll be back early this evening. Will you have dinner with me?'

'Back from where?' The words were out before she could stop them, and she cursed herself for appearing inquisitive.

'Sydney. I flew down yesterday.'

'Oh.'

'Shall we say seven?'

She wanted to say no, but a single monosyllabic acceptance left her lips of its own volition, and it was only after she had replaced the receiver that she cursed herself for being a fool in arranging to see him again.

The hours through the day dragged, and she was ready a good ten minutes before the appointed time, her nerves setting her stomach into an impossible knot as she waited. Twice she considered changing her attire, undecided whether the simple cream silk blouse and pencil-slim skirt were suitable for what he had in mind. A slight hysterical bubble burst in self-derisive mockery. What Ryan Marshall had in mind was undoubtedly to remove her clothing as skilfully and unobtrusively as possible!

His arrival created havoc with her finely-tuned senses, and the sight of his lengthy frame attired in an opened-necked black silk shirt and expensively-tailored cream trousers almost robbed her of the ability to speak.

In the car she sat in silence, and it was only when he turned from Chevron Island and headed towards Cronin Island that her worst fears were realised.

'We're dining at your home?'

Ryan's glance was swift and analytical. 'I prefer not to share your company with a room full of strangers.'

The butterflies in Natalie's stomach set up a frightening tattoo and she endeavoured to inject a steadiness into her voice. 'I think you'd better take me back to the hotel.'

The car slowed and turned into the wide sweeping driveway, coming to a halt outside the entrance. Carefully Ryan switched off the engine, then he turned towards her, resting an elbow on the steering wheel as he allowed his gaze to rove slowly over her expressive features.

Natalie forced her eyes to remain steady during that intense scrutiny, hating him for placing her in such an invidious position—hating herself equally for being so vulnerable.

'I have any number of female acquaintances with whom I can indulge a bedroom romp,' he informed her cynically, then pursued relentlessly, 'My housekeeper has prepared an excellent meal. The eating of it, in your company, is all I have in mind.'

'You expect me to believe that?'

'Get out of the car, Natalie.' His voice held a silky threat that sent shivers of apprehension slithering down the length of her spine, and she complied without so much as a word.

With a mounting sense of trepidation she preceded him through the wide panelled doors into the foyer, allowing herself to be led into a spacious lounge, and it wasn't until she had taken a few reviving sips of some excellent wine that she had the courage to take note of her surroundings.

The neutral clover-shaded carpet was thick-piled and luxurious, providing a perfect background for the dark laquered cane furniture whose soft-plumped cushions were covered in apricot silk. Expensive paintings adorned pale cream textured walls, and large sliding glass doors were smoke-tinted, providing privacy as well as acting as a filter for the strong Queensland sunlight.

'You have a beautiful home,' Natalie accorded sincerely, and glimpsed the faint sardonic cynicism in the tigerish eyes some distance from her own.

'Very politely spoken,' Ryan acknowledged with an edge of mockery. 'If I offer to show you the rest of it, doubtless you'll read some ulterior motive into the invitation.'

'Not at all,' she responded civilly. 'I'd find it a fascinating experience.'

Without a word he crossed the room, and taking the glass from her hand he placed it down on to a nearby glass-topped table. An eyebrow slanted in quizzical amusement as he glanced at her. 'Are you sure it's my home you're referring to?'

The wine had given her the necessary confidence to arm herself against him. 'Of course. I have your word that you have no ulterior motive in mind.'

His response was an echo of silent laughter, bringing an answering smile to her lips as she allowed herself to be led on a tour of inspection.

The house comprised three levels, two of which were evident from the front entrance. The lower level was at the rear overlooking the Nerang River, and it was in this large room that the party had been held. Slate-paved floors, brick and alternate timber feature walls provided a stunning background for the cane furniture, and sliding glass doors ran the entire length of one wall, opening out on to a paved courtyard where a magnificent swimming pool reposed, its translucent waters tinged a cool blue by exquisite tiling. The grounds were lit by inconspicuous lighting, revealing an outdoor barbecue area and perfect landscaping.

A formal dining room adjoined the lounge on the ground level, and opposite the main entrance foyer was an informal television lounge with comfortable sprawling chairs and settees, electronic stereo equipment, and a video recorder. There was also a study, a second informal dining room, beyond which was a kitchen containing every conceivable labour-saving electrical device, including a microwave oven.

The upper level comprised no fewer than five bedrooms, each with en suite facilities. The housekeeper's living quarters were a self-contained suite of rooms and were situated above the garages to the left of the house.

'Very impressive,' Natalie murmured as they reached the lounge. She had been conscious of Ryan's close proximity and aware of its effect on her equilibrium.

'Another drink?'

Dared she? There would be wine to accompany the meal, and somehow she had to get through the evening with all of her faculties intact. 'No, thank you,' she refused quietly. 'But don't let me stop you from having another.'

Ryan shook his head. 'Let's go in to dinner, shall we?'

Afterwards Natalie had no clear recollection of what she ate, other than that the food was excellent, the wine a palatable complement. They talked, touching on a wide variety of subjects, listened to music, and at midnight, in almost Cinderella fashion, she elected to leave.

Quite how she managed to find herself in Ryan's arms was a mystery, but it felt right to be there, and his mouth was gentle on hers, tasting the sweetness of her lips with a curious lightness that made her ache for more. Hardly aware of what she was doing, she let her arms creep up to clasp behind his neck as she unconsciously moved close against him.

A soft intake of breath was the only warning she received, then his mouth became hard and demanding, mastering her own in a kiss that was devastating. In a total annihilation of her senses, it left her weak-willed and malleable beneath his experienced hands, and when he finally released her she was barely able to stand.

'Home, I think,' Ryan decreed enigmatically, taking in her bemusement with a narrowed, slightly speculative gaze.

In the car outside her hotel he bestowed a brief hard kiss, then leaned across and opened her door.

To say Natalie floated through the entrance foyer was an understatement, and his image filled her dreams, haunting her through the following day until his phone call confirmed that he wanted to see her again—after hours spent convincing herself she was too young, too naïve—too *inexperienced*, for him to be the slightest bit interested.

They dated frequently—constantly, was perhaps more apt, and Natalie spent each day torn between the deep wealth of feeling Ryan was able to evoke, and the knowledge that it could never be anything more than a holiday romance. She managed to keep her head—barely. Each ensuing occasion became a subtle battle of willpower, and never before had she been made so shockingly aware just how easy it was to succumb to the moment, or to lose sight of the moral principles she considered so important.

The days flew, each signalling one less to be

spent in Ryan's company, and Natalie became filled with bitter-sweet agony as the close of her holiday drew near. The last evening commanded every ounce of strength she possessed, and she prepared for it carefully, taking an inordinate amount of time with her make-up, even going so far as to wear a new dress bought especially for the occasion.

When she stepped into the Ferrari her greeting was over-bright, her smile wide as she fastened the seatbelt. If Ryan noticed, he made no comment, and he eased the powerful car into the stream of traffic.

Natalie was too numb to take much notice of where they were going, and it was only when the car swept to a halt in the curved driveway that she realised he had brought her to his home. Given a choice, she would have opted for a large restaurant where the patronage and floorshow would provide an essential distraction. A quiet intimate candelit dinner might very well be her downfall!

The wine and the food were excellent, and she savoured each mouthful much as a condemned prisoner might regard his final meal. Coffee was served in the lounge, and it required both hands to hold the cup steady as he sipped the delicious brew.

'I'd like to thank you for making my holiday such an enjoyable one,' Natalie ventured evenly, amazed she hadn't stumbled over the words—despite having rehearsed the trite little phrase countless times throughout the day.

'Will you marry me?'

'It's been very kind of you to give up so much of your time,' she continued, then realisation dawned as the full intent of his words sank in. 'Would you mind—repeating that?' she uttered faintly, and glimpsed his silent laughter.

'Do I need to?'

Her eyes were wide and unblinking, and she could have sworn her heart stopped beating. 'I think so,' she said carefully.

Without a word Ryan extracted a small velvet jeweller's box, snapped open the lid, then slid the exquisite solitaire diamond on to the appropriate finger of her left hand.

'It's beautiful,' Natalie whispered, in awe of its magnificence. Large clear grey eyes regarded him seriously. 'Are you sure you want me to have it?'

'Shall I go down on bended knee and declare my unswerving devotion?' Ryan parried gently, holding her gaze.

'That might be expecting too much,' she began unsteadily. 'Although the temptation is almost irresistible.' A mischievous sparkle lit her eyes. 'Perhaps I should insist. I may never see you so humbled again.'

'Minx,' he murmured wryly, pulling her into his arms. I've a good mind to render a punishment that will have you begging for mercy!'

His mouth settled on hers with passionate intensity, searing as he branded his possession, and when she thought her lungs might burst his hold slackened.

'I think it's just as well I'm going home tomorrow,' Natalie voiced shakily as she rested her head against his hard chest. The thought of being apart from him, even for a day, seemed too much to bear.

'I'm flying down with you tomorrow to convince your father my intentions are honourable.' She sensed the smile she knew to be on his lips. 'Also to convince him that a short engagement is essential. Anything more than a week, and I'll be on the brink of insanity.'

'A *week*——'

'If it could be arranged in less time, believe me, it would be tomorrow.' He took her chin between thumb and forefinger, lifting it so she had no option but to look at him. 'I have no intention of allowing you out of my sight until we've exchanged our nuptial vows.' His eyes darkened with emotion, and his voice held cynical amusement. 'Left alone, you just might invent any number of reasons why we shouldn't marry. It's a risk I'm not prepared to take.' He lowered his head to kiss her—thoroughly, and when she surfaced again she was far too bemused to demur.

The week that followed retained a haziness that disallowed time for reflection, taken up as it was with countless arrangements, a trip to Melbourne for a wedding gown, time-consuming phone calls to friends, issuing invitations. Even the day itself held an elusive quality—Natalie could recall laughing, *crying*, displaying a gamut of emotions as she said goodbye to family and friends and boarded the private chartered jet with Ryan for an undisclosed destination.

An idyllic honeymoon on Green Island, off the coast from Cairns, was everything Natalie imagined it might be—and more. Ryan's love-making surpassed her wildest imagination, as beneath his skilful expertise she scaled the heights of emotional sensuality. She loved, believed herself to be loved in return, and was incapable of thinking anything could destroy her happiness.

Their return to Surfer's Paradise resulted in a seemingly endless stream of parties as Ryan's friends and business associates demanded an introduction to his bride.

A building contractor and developer, Ryan had a finger in several projects, among which numbered no fewer than three high-rise buildings along the coastal foreshore. The head of a well-established construction empire, he possessed an instinct to be in the right place at the right time, willing to take the calculated risks necessary to turn a successful business into a multi-million-dollar consortium. A respected member of the community, he was on the board of directors of more than one corporation, and socially much in demand.

It was at one such party that Natalie came into contact with Simone Vesey—a dark-haired, creamy-skinned model whose tall willowy frame was a human clothes peg for several designers, her classical features photographed and included in several of the world's leading fashion magazines.

Whether by invitation or design, Simone was an inclusion at every function Natalie and Ryan attended, and it didn't take any imagination at all to understand that the glamorous woman was a veritable man-eater, or that her prime target was the highly desirable Ryan Marshall. His new bride was regarded as easily dismissable, and little more bothersome than a tiresome insect!

Well-meaning matrons hinted that Ryan was a bit of a rake—reformed, of course, with the advent of his marriage—and if gossip could be relied upon, his past had been anything but exemplary.

It hadn't taken long for the first seeds of doubt to take root in Natalie's mind. Ryan's dedication to work was something she could understand, and although he always endeavoured to be home for dinner when they were not entertaining or being entertained, there were occasions when business intervened. At first she took little notice of the phone calls saying he would be late, not to wait dinner as he had to entertain a business associate.

Simone's subtle innuendoes became a steady drip of poison, conspiring to make Natalie feel insecure, resulting in several pleas to lessen their social obligations—something Ryan resisted, then as she began to persist he grew increasingly impatient, and the arguments began.

With no friend in whom to confide her misgivings, Natalie began to view each social occasion as a silent battle—more a war of nerves, with Simone steadily emerging the winner.

After one terrible argument Natalie found it impossible to bear Ryan's intolerance a moment longer and quietly packed a bag and left, returning home to Casterton where, sworn to secrecy, her father and Andrea had disavowed any knowledge of her whereabouts.

The discovery that she might be pregnant came within weeks of her return home, and despite all opposition she chose to keep Ryan in ignorance, destroying unopened the letters that arrived for forwarding, and a month later she instructed a solicitor in Melbourne to write to Ryan on her behalf stating that there was no possibility of a reconciliation and that she desired no further contact.

Choosing to lead a quiet restrained life, almost to the point of seclusion, she managed to get through the months prior to Michelle's birth, and afterwards she had made the child her reason for living, showering love and attention with enviable maternal devotion.

CHAPTER FOUR

THE first leg of the flight was over. Natalie freshened up and attended to Michelle's needs, then rejoined Ryan in the airport lounge.

'Ready?'

Too choked to utter so much as a word, she merely nodded, and it wasn't until they were on the tarmac and about to board the jet that she dared trust herself to speak.

'I won't make a willing captive,' she warned in a dark undertone.

'My dear Natalie,' he drawled, sparing her a mocking glance, 'I didn't for one minute imagine you would.'

Inside the small cabin she sank into a seat and settled Michelle, checking their seatbelts, and was all too aware of Ryan's presence directly opposite.

The small plane began taxiing out towards the runway, its passage smooth.

'How are you going to explain my sudden return to the Marshall household?' Natalie queried with a note of defiance. The ruthless set of his compelling features was daunting, yet something goaded her on, blotting out all rational thought. 'Your current—er——' she paused with seeming delicacy, 'girl-friend isn't going to like the fact that your ex-wife is about to be reinstated.'

The silence inside the cabin seemed to reverberate until it became almost a tangible entity.

'*Ex*-wife, Natalie?' he demanded with silky detachment.

The screaming pitch of the jet's engines

precluded an immediate reply, and she waited until they were airborne before offering to comment.

'We've been apart for three years,' she defended. 'That constitutes a separation.'

'I prefer to call it an estrangement.'

Natalie let out a heartfelt sigh. 'So what explanation is going to be given in view of our supposed reconciliation? In the interests of feasibility we should both stick to the same story.'

'My private life is my own,' Ryan asserted irrefutably, and she didn't doubt he could fend off the most curious of queries with a chilling stare, whereas she would founder like a gasping fish in the face of the more formidable of his acquaintances.

'And Michelle?' she persisted. 'Her presence will doubtless raise more than an eyebrow or two.'

'I don't give a damn.'

A tiny devil tempted her further. 'Suppose it's implied she's not your child?'

A muscle tensed along his jaw, and the blazing glance he threw her was filled with icy rage. 'Be thankful for Michelle's presence. If it weren't for her, I'd thrash you to within an inch of your life,' he vowed mercilessly.

'Jealous, Ryan?'

His expression was implacable as he put a rein on his temper. 'There will come an hour when we're alone,' he inclined pitilessly. 'Will you be so brave then, I wonder?'

'What do you intend?' she muttered, hating him as the butterflies in her stomach began an erratic tattoo. 'Am I to suffer some torture of the damned now you've found me again?'

'Is that what you think?'

'I feel like a recalcitrant child hauled before the headmistress for having dared played truant from school,' she vented defensively, and he laughed, a deep-throated sound totally devoid of humour.

'I'm not sure I approve the comparison,' Ryan acknowledged dryly.

'I would hardly expect you to,' Natalie sighed with resignation, and turned to check that Michelle hadn't attempted to tamper with her seatbelt.

The little tot was happily engrossed with her favourite toy and appeared oblivious to everything else. An amenable child, she was used to amusing herself and adored travelling, rarely becoming fractious whenever Natalie ventured out—which wasn't often.

Like a sleek silver bird, the jet steadily transported Natalie towards another world, and she suppressed a shiver of apprehension as to whether she could cope with the faster paced lifestyle, the constant social round of parties and formal dinners—more important, the people who made up Ryan's circle of friends and acquaintances. The inherent backstabbing and one-upmanship beneath the thin veneer of charm was a factor she found difficult to condone.

'Second thoughts?'

She turned at the sound of that deep voice, and deliberately avoided Ryan's penetrating gaze. A sense of fatalism invaded her bones, and she was unable to suppress the feeling that she was embarking on a journey from which there could be no return.

The first opalescent glow of dusk was beginning to tinge the early evening sky as the small jet circled Coolangatta airport prior to its descent.

For the remainder of the flight Ryan had chosen to devote most of his attention to his daughter, who, contrary to Natalie's expressed will to become fractious, had done little else but laugh and indulge in an endless patter of barely comprehensible chatter. For all the notice Natalie's presence received, she might as well not even have been there! A secret part of her silently screamed at Michelle's downright fickle behaviour. Damn Ryan! He possessed the power to charm any female regardless of age, and Michelle was no exception.

An elegant Daimler stood in solitary splendour near the entrance to the car park, and Natalie evinced little surprise when Ryan moved towards the opulent vehicle and unlocked the passenger door.

'What happened to the Ferrari?' It was an idle query and meant to convey sarcasm.

'I still have it,' Ryan answered dryly, shooting her a dark glance. 'However, you'll have to agree that it's hardly a suitable vehicle in which to transport a young child, plus luggage.'

She uttered a deprecatory laugh. 'I suppose Jenkins uses the Daimler to do the shopping.'

'As a matter of fact, he does.'

'My God!' she declared with pious disregard. 'You've become even more of an autocratic plutocrat than ever!'

An eyebrow slanted in her direction. 'Are you going to hold it against me?'

How could she? He had worked long hard hours from an early age, using what capital he earned to invest in property, then building, selling, achieving capital gains for reinvestment. From employing one labourer, he now headed one of the largest construction companies on the Gold Coast. Ryan Marshall was a self-made man who deserved his hard-earned success.

Michelle began to cry, the first pitiful whimper

rapidly becoming an indignant wail that refused to be soothed.

At Ryan's faintly raised eyebrow, Natalie had to forcibly restrain a self-satisfied smile. It would do him good to realise his daughter wasn't all sweetness and light!

'She's hungry,' she explained, trying to console the upset infant without success. 'And apart from a short doze on the plane, she hasn't had her usual afternoon sleep.'

'We'll be home in thirty minutes.' Ryan slid in behind the wheel and ignited the engine, easing the large vehicle out into the steady stream of traffic moving northwards along the main highway.

'Young children are sticklers for routine,' Natalie said dryly. 'It's fifteen minutes after her mealtime. I doubt she'll last half an hour without something. There's a few pieces of fruit and a packet of cereal biscuits in my bag,' she told him, looking for it, and seeing it was neither at her feet nor on the rear seat. 'Damn!' The exclamation fell from her lips without thought. 'You must have stowed it in the boot with everything else.'

Ryan threw her a sharp darting glance. 'I'll pull over as soon as I can get into the left lane. Good grief!' he exclaimed as Michelle let out a yell. 'Is she usually this noisy?'

Natalie's smile was a mere facsimile, and she ventured sweetly, 'As far as obstinacy and getting her own way are concerned, she's every bit her father's daughter.'

Five minutes later Michelle had finished a banana and was happily munching a cereal biscuit as the car sped swiftly through Burleigh on the main coastal highway.

It seemed all too soon that numerous high-rise buildings encroached the darkening skyline, a myriad winking lights providing a panoramic fairyland that competed with brightly flashing neon as they reached the outskirts of the tourist resort.

'The Chevron have added a new accommodation tower to their complex,' Ryan told her as they passed a brightly lit entrance, and seconds later they negotiated the Chevron bridge, slowing imperceptibly to adapt to a lower speed limit.

As they reached Cronin Island the Daimler swept through the gates and the illuminated driveway cast shadows over the splendid landscaped grounds as Ryan brought the car to a halt before the impressive entrance.

'I've instructed Martha to serve dinner at eight,' he told her as he slid out and crossed to open her door. 'I imagine that will give you time to feed, bath and put Michelle down for the night?'

Natalie felt her stomach muscles tighten at the thought *bed* evoked—more particularly, *his* bed, and the fact that he would insist she share it.

'In a strange house she may not settle immediately,' she warned, cradling the little girl close as she stepped out from the car. 'I'd like a shower, and a change of clothes, if I may?'

'This is your home, Natalie,' Ryan reminded her dryly, and she cast him a sceptical glance.

'No,' she corrected evenly. 'It's where you're forcing me to live. This grandiose—mansion was never intended to be anyone's *home*. It's an elegantly appointed showplace in which to entertain and impress, with never a speck of dust in evidence or a cushion out of place.'

His expression was deliberately enigmatic. 'Shall we go inside? I imagine Martha and Jenkins are anxious to renew their friendship.'

Natalie mounted the few steps ahead of him,

summoning a slight smile as the solid oak-panelled door swung open. Jenkins' usually solemn features relaxed with genuine pleasure, and he ventured cordially,

'It's good to have you back, if I may say so miss.'

'You haven't changed, Jenkins,' she told him, unable to still the dancing light in her eyes. Possessing a droll sense of humour that never surfaced in the presence of guests, the manservant and his wife were more friends than employees, running Ryan's home with enviable efficiency and loving care. Doubtless he had been given a christian name, but Natalie had never heard it, and even Martha referred to her husband by his surname.

'You'll find everything just as you left it,' Jenkins revealed, regarding Michelle with undisguised interest. 'Martha has prepared a room opposite the main suite for the little one, and she has a meal ready, whenever you wish to feed her.'

'Thank you,' Natalie responded gratefully, aware that Ryan had come to stand beside her.

'Smooth flight, I presume?' Jenkins enquired of his employer. 'There were three calls. I've left details in your study.'

'I'll attend to them later,' Ryan drawled, taking hold of Natalie's elbow. 'First, we need to get this young lady settled into her new home.'

'Delightful little thing, isn't she?' the older man observed with a smile. 'I daresay she's hungry.'

'She was,' Ryan said dryly, and Jenkins chuckled as he shot Natalie a conspiratorial grin.

'Cried, did she?'

'With earsplitting velocity!'

'It's something must young children do when they're tired and hungry,' Natalie defended, trying to extricate herself from her husband's grasp. 'Tell Martha I'll be ready to feed Michelle in about five minutes. I'll just wash her face and hands first.'

Jenkins was right, she perceived on reaching the upper floor. Nothing had changed. Not even the colour of the towels placed in the bathroom. Almost as if in the presence of a ghost, she shivered as memories returned to haunt her. Just by closing her eyes it was all too easy to remember those few laughter love-filled months she had spent in this house, loving and being loved as she'd never dreamed possible. Beneath Ryan's infinite expertise she'd learnt to shed every last inhibition, incredulous that any two people had the right to be so happy. Even then she had been aware that one day the beautiful bubble might burst, but nothing had prepared her for the resultant pain, the devastating agony that followed in its wake. Like a wounded animal she had run away to hide until the scars could heal.

Now, coming here had merely made her more aware of the reason she had left. How could she live in the same house as Ryan, hating him as she did? When every waking minute she wanted to hurt him as he had hurt her? It could only result in a fiasco, with Michelle caught in the middle. A child should be surrounded with love, guided by discipline, not the means by which two people were flung together.

Dear Lord! she groaned audibly. Ryan had ensured he held all the winning cards. There would be no second escape.

Michelle's disgruntled whimper brought Natalie out of her reverie, and with a determined smile she attended to the little tot's needs before scooping her back into her arms, then she returned downstairs.

There was no sign of Ryan, and Natalie breathed a sigh of relief as she made her way to the kitchen, experiencing a slight wariness at the initial meeting with Martha.

The faint coolness soon evaporated as the older woman clucked and exclaimed over Michelle, and whatever her private thoughts regarding Natalie's flight and subsequent return, they were carefully hidden.

'She's adorable!' she smiled.

'Most of the time,' Natalie acceded as she helped her daughter scrape the last of her vegetables from the plate. The little girl began to rock back and forth, signifying her desire to leave the table.

'I'll take her upstairs for a bath,' Natalie decided, lifting the child into her arms. 'Then, with the help of some warm milk, she'll probably go off to sleep.'

Michelle waved her hand when they reached the door, much to Martha's delight, then in a fit of unaccustomed shyness the toddler buried her head against her mother's neck.

Bathtime invariably involved a variety of splashing games, and this evening was no exception. Natalie cast a rueful glance at her dampened clothes, and shook her head as Michelle attempted to send another spray of water her way.

'That's enough, my girl!' she remonstrated with a grin, plucking the protesting child from the water.

Michelle emitted a peal of laughter as she was enveloped in a large fluffy towel, wriggling for all she was worth in an attempt to prolong her bedtime.

Slipping on vest and nightgown required split-second timing for success. 'Rascal!' Natalie scolded when the task was completed. 'Now, into your nice bed with Teddy, while I go fetch your milk. Okay?'

Halfway down the stairs she met Ryan, and there was nothing she could do about her sudden erratic heartbeat at the sight of him. Gone was the formal jacket, and the three top buttons of his shirt were undone, revealing a glimpse of golden curling hair between the vee of blue silk. Her breathing became faintly uneven and she steeled herself against the dynamic masculinity he exuded, hating the way all her nerve-ends prickled in sheer awareness of his presence.

'You look like a drowned kitten,' he drawled, subjecting her to a lingering scrutiny that paused over-long on the damp patches on her blouse.

Too late Natalie remembered the absence of a bra, and as if he could read her mind Ryan uttered a soft sensual laugh that brought colour flying to her cheeks. She was suddenly aware of damp tendrils of hair that had escaped the smooth knot pinned on top of her head, the faint clean smell of baby powder that clung to her clothes, and with a muttered exclamation she hastily brushed past him.

Damn! she cursed silently as she made her way to the kitchen. Her hands were decidedly shaky as she filled the clean beaker Martha had left beside the small saucepan of warm milk. She felt so tense and overwrought it wasn't funny!

When she reached Michelle's bedroom it was to find Ryan sitting on the side of the bed intent on amusing the little girl. With an easy laugh he extracted the tot from the bed and carried her to a nearby chair.

'I usually sit her on the floor when she drinks,' Natalie said stiltedly, and received a wry glance as he complied by placing Michelle down on to the carpet. 'She's very good usually, and rarely spills a drop.'

'Am I a usurper in this domain?'

'How can you be, when this is your home?'

'Ours, Natalie,' he drawled, and she cast him a withering glance.

'Don't remind me!'

Michelle seemed lost to the task of finishing her milk, and already her eyes looked heavy, the lids drooping in tiredness.

'Go and have your shower,' Ryan bade quietly. 'I'll stay with her until she's asleep.'

'What if she cries?' Natalie asked doubtfully, and he arched an eyebrow in quizzical amusement.

'Afraid I won't be able to cope? There's always Martha to come to my rescue.'

'In that case,' she responded sweetly, 'I'll leave you to it.' She blew Michelle a kiss, then turned and left the room.

In the main suite she extracted clean underwear and a slim-fitting dress of crease-resistant lilac silk, then moved through to the bathroom.

The warm needle-spray had a soothing effect, and she stayed longer than necessary before turning off the water and stepping from the shower stall. Five minutes later she was dressed, and after applying a minimum of make-up she crossed the hallway and checked on Michelle before descending the stairs.

'Shall I pour you a drink?'

Natalie moved into the lounge and selected a solitary armchair before sinking into it with more than a little trepidation. An elegant crystal glass part filled with light amber liquid was held in one hand, and Ryan looked formidable and slightly menacing.

'A Martini, please.' Heaven knew she needed

something to bolster her morale! A slanted eyebrow greeted the request, and when she took the glass from his hand she swallowed the contents within minutes, extending it to be refilled without batting an eyelid.

Already the painful knot of nerves inside her stomach was beginning to relax, lending a false calmness to her manner.

'I imagine we're supposed to be frightfully civil,' Natalie began politely. 'Can you suggest a safe topic of conversation we can pursue? I'm afraid I've lost touch with the current political situation, and I can't recall a thing to relate that might be of interest.'

'It would help if you stopped regarding me as an animal about to pounce on its prey,' Ryan drawled, and she effected a faint grimace.

'But you will, won't you?' she declared wryly. 'You're not a man to be crossed lightly, and I've no doubt you'll exact some form of revenge.' She took a generous sip, amazed at the lucidity the alcohol appeared to have in transferring thoughts to words! 'Three years, Ryan,' she pondered deliberately, subjecting him to an unwavering scrutiny. 'I imagine a bevy of delectable women have vied for your company, eager to assuage any—er—loneliness.' Even the mere thought of that lean hard body making love to any other nubile female froze her features into a dispassionate mask. 'I doubt my absence has even been noticed.'

'Don't try my patience too far,' he warned silkily. 'I can promise you won't like the consequences.'

'I'm trembling already.' The sarcasm was an echo of the truth, and he knew it.

'So you should,' he opined softly, and Natalie stood quickly to her feet.

'I've lost my appetite. In fact, I'm sure any food would stick in my throat.' She turned, and had taken no more than three steps when hard hands caught hold of her arms, halting her flight, and Ryan swung her round to face him in one easy movement.

'Oh no, you don't,' he drawled, and his eyes narrowed fractionally as she began to struggle. 'Be still, for the love of heaven!' The directive was explosive, and his fingers bit into her soft flesh.

'You're hurting me!' Her bitterness wasn't feigned, and with an angry oath he released his grip.

'Three years ago I could have strangled you without the slightest hesitation,' he revealed with wry cynicism.

Natalie swallowed compulsively. 'How do you think I felt,' she began a trifle shakily, 'when I discovered the "loving husband" image you projected was just that—an image?' Her eyes filled with anger. 'An elusive non-existent entity,' she brooded, gaining courage as she met his steady enigmatic gaze. 'I was an easy target—a real innocent babe.' A soundless laugh of derision left her lips. 'You had it all, Ryan, and I, poor fool, thought it was love!' An edge of mockery entered her voice. 'Amazing that you proposed marriage— something, I gathered from the ever-lovely Simone, you'd never been known to offer in the past.'

His expression was inscrutable, and the edge of his mouth lifted in a gesture of sardonic cynicism. 'It didn't occur to you to regard Simone's revelations in the light of "Hell hath no fury like a woman scorned"?'

Her gaze was incredibly steady. 'At first—yes. I wasn't too naïve not to recognise that she would go to any lengths to get you. If it had been just

Simone——' she faltered slightly, then went on, 'But there were others only too willing to testify to having shared a torrid affair.' Her faint laugh sounded slightly off-key. 'I was surrounded by vicious, envious women intent on pressing home their painful barbs. I was even given proof,' she disclosed dispassionately. 'The opportunity to discover for myself that one of your supposed "business dinners" was nothing less than a cover for an——' she paused, then added with contrived delicacy—'extra-marital liaison with Simone.'

It seemed an age before Ryan spoke, and she shivered at the icy rage evident beneath the silkiness of his voice. 'By heaven, you seem bent on inviting the wrath of God—whose patience is doubtless more provident than mine!'

For a heartstopping moment Natalie thought he meant to strike her, and she drained her glass in one long swallow, then carefully placed it down on a nearby table. 'If you'll excuse me, I'll go upstairs.'

'We'll eat dinner—together,' Ryan insisted hardily, quelling her retort with a pitiless glare. 'You had almost nothing for breakfast, and hardly touched any lunch.' He subjected her slim curves to an analytical scrutiny, and muttered with exasperation, 'God knows, you're little more than skin and bone.'

'Thanks!' she acknowledged bitterly. 'I've never been voluptuous.'

'A few weeks of Martha's cooking will soon add essential kilos,' he declared brutally, leading her towards the dining room, and when she was seated he uncorked the wine and filled her glass.

'*Salute.*'

Natalie didn't acknowledge the mocking toast, and merely sipped at the contents of her glass as she viewed the variety of covered dishes on the table. Gleaming silver and fine bone china reposed on white damask, and Martha had arranged an attractive floral centrepiece that was a perfect foil for the exquisite candelabrum.

Without reference to her taste, Ryan placed a portion from each dish on to her plate, and when she toyed with it, added a sharp admonition.

'I'm not a child!' she snapped resentfully.

His glance speared her mercilessly. 'Then stop behaving like one.'

'You can't force me to eat.'

For a few fateful seconds they warred a silent battle, then Ryan said quietly, 'Martha has gone to a lot of trouble to ensure that your first evening home is an enjoyable one. If you don't eat, she'll take it as a personal affront to her culinary skills.'

'Bravo,' Natalie said bleakly. 'I have little option but to concede defeat.' Without a further word she picked up the appropriate cutlery and set about doing justice to the food on her plate.

Every mouthful seemed to require painstaking effort, and she was conscious that it was taking her an inordinate amount of time to complete the meal. When it was finally over, she almost slumped back in her seat with relief. The nerves in her stomach were beginning to play havoc with her digestion, and there was nothing she wanted more than to leave the room and Ryan's hateful company.

Summoning a taut smile, she folded her napkin and rose to her feet. 'If you'll excuse me, I'll for go coffee.'

'In such a hurry to go to bed, Natalie?'

Her insides began to shake, but she managed to keep her voice steady. 'We've been travelling since early morning. I'm tired.' And scared stiff, she added silently. Not only of Ryan, but her own wayward emotions.

'Just be sure which bed you occupy,' he warned with dangerous softness.

'I've been there, and back—remember?' she reminded him with a trace of weary bitterness, and without a further word she left the room, crossing the spacious foyer to the stairs.

In the main suite she entered the bathroom and removed her make-up, then brushed her teeth and picked up the brush to render her customary number of strokes, following a ritual so familiar it required no conscious thought.

Retracing her steps to the bedroom, she saw that her suitcase had disappeared, and investigation revealed that Martha had competently restored its contents to one of the walk-in wardrobes.

Selecting a nightgown, Natalie removed her clothes and donned the filmy creation—noting with wry resignation that the utilitarian cotton shifts she had packed had been successfully hidden—doubtless by the romantically-inclined housekeeper. Anything further from a romantic reconciliation couldn't be imagined!

The large bed seemed to mock her silently, and she closed her eyes in an effort to shut out the sight of it and all it signified. She couldn't slip beneath the sheets and lie waiting for Ryan to materalise—it simply wasn't possible! And where are you going to run to? a tiny imp jeered. There's nowhere he won't find you within this huge house, and any thought of going into the grounds would only invite disaster!

With the actions of an automaton, Natalie crossed to the bedside cabinet and switched on the lamp before closing the main overhead light.

A strange restlessness made it impossible for her to settle to anything, and without being aware of it she began to pace back and forth, oblivious to all but an overwhelming feeling of desperation. If it wasn't too ridiculous a comparison, she felt like a condemned prisoner awaiting final condemnation!

Dear heaven, if only he'd hurry up, so that it could be over and done with! But it was all part of a game, a cruel play on her emotions. As revenge, however subtle, it was totally effective, for she couldn't remember ever being such a quivering mass of nerves!

Damn Ryan—*damn* him to hell! she muttered inaudibly as anger rose to the fore, filling her with towering rage. Who did he think he was—a feudal lord? And she a shivering grateful waif? The devil she'd wait for his appearance!

The soft swish of silk was the only sound to signify her movement as she swept from the room, and without hesitation she made for a guestroom at the furthest end of the hall.

Cool satin sheets felt inordinately luxurious, and she laid her head against the pillow, closing her eyes in the hope that sleep would overtake her.

It didn't, of course, and she tossed restlessly, her head filled with too many haunting memories to induce somnolence.

Natalie wasn't sure when Ryan entered the room, only that some sixth sense warned he was there, and she watched in mesmerised fascination as he moved toward the bed.

In the semi-darkness he towered large and infinitely formidable, his features appearing harsh as a thin stream of moonlight highlighted the broad planes and angles of his face.

'You little fool,' he drawled in a dangerously

quiet voice. Without the slightest effort he pulled back the covers and lifted her into his arms.

'Put me down!' she hissed vehemently, and began pummelling his hard chest with her fists. 'I'm quite capable of walking!'

In the main suite he allowed her to slide to her feet, and she gave a silent cry of pain as his hands caught her shoulders in a bruising grip.

'Why make things worse for yourself?' he rasped, his eyes dark with anger, and Natalie retaliated without thought to the consequences.

'Did you honestly expect to find me *here*?' She cast her glance wildly round the luxuriously appointed room, and her voice shook with rage. 'My God! What do you think I am? A masochist?'

Ryan's expression subtly changed to assume sardonic cynicism. 'I retain a vivid memory of a sweet biddable girl who became a witching wanton in my arms.'

She suddenly had great difficulty in swallowing, and it took considerable effort to meet and hold his gaze. 'That girl grew up,' she offered steadily. 'You saw to it—personally.'

His eyes narrowed fractionally, and she sensed the latent anger lying dormant beneath the surface of his control. 'Are you going to fight me every inch of the way?'

'What else do you expect?'

'Not compliance,' he admitted with an edge of mockery, and Natalie raised solemn grey eyes to his, taking in the hard planes of his chiselled features as she sought to gauge his mood.

'You intend that I shall.' It was a statement that hardly conceded defeat, and his mouth gave a wry twist.

'You know it.'

'Why?' she demanded simply. 'What possible

satisfaction can you derive?'

'What would you know about my satisfaction?' Ryan taunted, and his hands impelled her close so that she was made all too aware of his arousal.

'I don't like being a subject of lust!'

His warm breath fanned her temple, teasing loose a few curling blonde tendrils. 'You have the damnedest way of deploying words. Why not relax?'

'So that it will make you feel better when you take me?' She met his gaze steadily. 'Sorry, but I'm not that charitable.'

Gold eyes gleamed with inimical anger. 'By heaven,' he breathed ominously, 'you'd tempt the devil himself!'

Natalie drew a deep unsteady breath, and managed to keep her voice even with the greatest difficulty. 'What will it prove? Other than your need to exact some form of revenge?'

'What in hell would you suggest?' he demanded, and his hands tightened over her delicate shoulder bones, making her wince with pain. 'I have an irresistible urge to make you pay,' he muttered with dangerous softness, giving her an ungentle shake, and her eyes blazed with bitter anger.

'Do you imagine I haven't?' She felt sick with the tumult of her emotions. 'It wasn't easy for me to return home and admit to a failed marriage, nor was it exactly a picnic being pregnant without a husband's support. I cursed you a thousand times when my body was racked with the agony of trying to give birth, until the doctors decided on a Caesarian.' Her grey eyes clouded with remembered pain. 'For more than two years I've lived with the fear that you might discover Michelle's existence, knowing that if you did, I'd be forced to part with her.' She gave a choked laugh. 'God knows, Ryan—I've *paid*!'

His hands tightened into an excruciating grip that made her cry out, and with a muffled oath he thrust her from him. A muscle tensed along his jaw, and she shivered in the force of his barely suppessed fury.

'Dammit, Natalie,' he swore with explosive force, 'what do you want from me? Remorse for getting you pregnant? For not being there like any other expectant father?' His eyes became bleak with bitterness. 'You didn't give me the opportunity.'

'And if I had?' she demanded with agonised incredulity. 'You'd have had a team of highly proficient lawyers extricate Michelle before I'd regained the strength to fight you!'

For interminable seconds Ryan just stood there regarding her in total silence, his features an inscrutable mask, then he gave an inaudible mocking laugh. 'Your opinion of me isn't very flattering.'

Natalie had the greatest difficulty in swallowing the lump in her throat. 'I haven't had reason to think otherwise.'

'Yet you're here,' Ryan reminded her sardonically. 'At my insistence.' His eyes lanced her to the bone. 'Pleasant dreams,' he said with quiet mockery, and turning away he moved towards the door to leave the room without so much as a backward glance.

CHAPTER FIVE

NATALIE woke to hear the muted sound of running water, indicative of someone occupying the shower in the adjoining bathroom. A glance at her watch revealed that it was barely six, and she gave an inaudible groan before burying her head beneath the pillow.

Seconds later she was fully awake and mentally alert. There was only one person who would utilise the bedroom's en suite facilities, and her eyes flew to the empty space beside her, seeing at once the cast-back covers and the imprint on the pillow.

'You slept here!' she accused on a note of hysteria the instant Ryan appeared through the doorway.

He looked fresh and compellingly vital, his muscle frame whipcord-hard and aggressively male, the towel hitched carelessly about his hips a mere concession to the bounds of decency.

'My room, my bed,' he drawled with imperturbable calm. 'Where else would I sleep?'

'There are other rooms,' she hissed in outrage, and catching the direction of his slow lazy appraisal she hastily drew the sheets up to her chin.

'And give Jenkins and Martha reason to suspect our reconciliation might be a sham?' he enquired with studied mockery.

'The conventions must be observed at all costs,' Natalie sneered with noted sarcasm, her mind in a turmoil at the thought of having spent the night in the same bed with him. Worse, to have been unaware of it.

'You're here to stay,' Ryan stated brusquely. 'The sooner you come to terms with that fact, the better.'

'Even though I find it utterly hateful?'

His expression assumed cynical mockery. 'Consider the alternative.' He turned and walked with pantherish grace towards a large capacious wardrobe and slid open the door, extracted essential items of clothing, then proceeded to dress.

Natalie quickly averted her gaze from his lithe muscled torso, a faint tinge of pink colouring her cheeks as she caught his soft chuckle.

'You can look now,' he murmured sardonically, and she swung round to face him, a fiery sparkle kindling her eyes.

'Will you please get out of here.'

He buttoned his shirt and tucked it into snug-fitting suede trousers, his expression lazily amused. 'Why?'

Fury erupted inside her like molten lava. 'Because I want to get out of bed, that's why!'

One eyebrow rose in mocking query. 'My dear Natalie—*modesty*?' A slight smile tugged the corners of his sensually-moulded mouth. 'After three years of marriage, and having borne my child?'

'We lived as man and wife for only three *months*, and you know it!' she blazed, and his eyes narrowed fractionally.

'A fact I intend to remedy before long.'

'I won't let you.' Fine words, when she didn't stand a chance against his superior strength, or the degree of sensual expertise at his command.

As if he knew the pattern of her thoughts he gave a slight smile. 'Do you really think you could stop me?'

'No,' she answered steadily. 'But I doubt if you'd enjoy making love to a block of ice.'

His hard intent stare played havoc with her composure, and she stifled a silent scream at the strength of purpose in those chilling depths.

With slow unhurried movements he unbuttoned his shirt, pulling it free from the waistband of his trousers, and when his fingers released the zip she burst into incredulous speech.

'What do you think you're doing?' Her eyes widened into large stormy pools that relayed fear as he casually thrust his discarded clothes on to a nearby chair, and her throat constricted, choking off any sound that might otherwise have been emitted.

He moved with indolent ease towards the bed, his dark gaze hard and unwavering, and she couldn't have looked away if her life depended on it.

'Don't—please!' The words were wrung from her throat in a tortured whisper, and she cried out as he reached for the sheet and tore it from her grasp.

His appraisal of her thinly-clad body in its silken gown was indolently insolent, and she scrambled across the width of the bed, only to be caught and held with dismaying ease.

Natalie began to struggle in earnest, twisting to lash out at him, pummelling the sinewy shoulders, his ribs, chest—anywhere she could manage to connect her flailing fists.

Without any effort at all Ryan caught first one arm, then the other, and held them above her head.

'You unspeakable fiend!'

Topaz eyes glittered with latent anger. 'Let's see how long you can remain an icicle, my sweet wife,' he drawled with hateful cynicism, and Natalie cried out as he put a hand to the neckline of her nightgown and ripped it cleanly to its hem.

'You can't do this,' she whispered, her voice coming out in an agonised rush, and he took hold of her chin, forcing it high.

'Destroy a dispensable bit of cloth?' His mouth moved to form a wry smile. 'There are several to replace it, in drawers, exactly where you left them.' A slow sweeping glance took in every inch of her, and she writhed beneath its analytical appraisal.

'I hate——' The words were lost as his mouth crushed hers, bruising in its intensity, and she groaned inaudibly as he forced her lips apart to sear the sweetness within. It was a brutal invasion of her senses which numbed and shocked, and she was scarcely aware when the pressure eased and took on a persuasive quality.

With a slow featherlight touch, Ryan began to caress each vulnerable hollow, trailing his lips along a familiar path that had in the past led her towards an ultimate explosion of ecstasy.

Natalie closed her eyes and willed her body not to respond as his tongue teased an exploratory circle of one rosy-peaked breast before tantalising the other. All her fine body hairs prickled in awareness of his sensual arousal, and her whole body began to vibrate with an emotion she was unable to control.

Not content, his mouth travelled back to cover her own, and this time there was a wealth of seduction in his touch as he employed subtle persuasion in a manner that was impossible to ignore.

A slow ache started in the region of her stomach and steadily spread to her loins, and she threshed restlessly against the encompassing passion that ran like quicksilver through her veins, totally at variance with her brain and her desperate resolve not to succumb.

Like a maestro Ryan played the delicate sensory pulse-beats with virtuoso mastery, exacting the very response she had sworn not to give, and Natalie was scarcely aware of her voice begging the release only his body could assuage until the climax had been reached and subsided, and she lay spent beside him.

'I loathe you,' she declared shakily, trying to move away without success.

'Be quiet.' It was a husky admonition delivered close to her ear, and his hand lifted to smooth back the length of her hair in a strangely gentle gesture.

Of their own volition her lips began to tremble. 'Damn you—*damn* you,' she whispered with impotent rage, the hate inside rising to give her eyes a fiery sparkle. She felt tormented, *tortured*, and most damning of all—betrayed. 'You planned that—seduction scene, didn't you?' she voiced bitterly, hating him with a depth of feeling that was vaguely frightening.

'Yes,' Ryan revealed with brutal frankness, and grasping hold of her chin he forced her to look at him. 'Hate me for it if you must, but there was no other way.'

'You could have given me time,' Natalie cried, sorely tried, and glimpsed his wry smile.

'Providing provocation, but unwilling to deliver?' There was mocking cynicism evident in the compelling features so close to her own. 'I won't be manipulated, Natalie—not even by you.'

'That's a horrible thing to say,' she said in slightly strangled tones, and his eyes narrowed speculatively.

'Yet you would take pleasure in deliberately baiting me, withholding so-called sexual favours,' he drawled. 'Something, I imagine, you'd regard as a form of divine punishment.'

She was goaded to retaliate, and she did so with scarcely a thought to the possible consequences. 'And being the egotistical male that you are, it has to be your hand that wields the power—like some sort of human god!'

'My equation of sexual equality doesn't permit otherwise.'

'Oh, go to hell!' she muttered impotently, unable to deal with the force of his masculinity a moment longer.

'You can fight me as often, and for as long as you like,' Ryan intimated heartlessly. 'Just remember I always intend to be the victor.'

The tip of her tongue edged its way along her lower lip in a purely nervous gesture. 'What if you're wrong?' Ridiculous to imagine a man of Ryan's calibre could ever make a false judgment! 'Would you concede defeat?'

'Elaborate, Natalie,' he drawled, and her gaze was remarkably steady.

'What if things don't work out?' she queried bravely. 'Or suppose neither treatment nor surgery for my father is successful? What then?'

'If you mean—will I let you go? The answer is no.'

'How can you say that?' she demanded. 'John's life-span is limited. You know it as well as I do.'

The pressure on her chin increased, and her eyes became stormy at the pain he was inflicting.

'The bond that ties us together is Michelle,' he told her with brooding savagery. 'Anything to do with your father's health is merely incidental.'

'So you won't——'

'Tolerate divorce,' he finished silkily, adding, 'or any form of separation. Be sure of it.'

'But that's a——'

'Lifetime sentence,' he elucidated with chilling finality, and Natalie shivered involuntarily.

'You're nothing less than an unfeeling monster!'

'Whom you hate, eh?'

'Utterly,' she responded succinctly, and incurred his mocking amusement.

'It wasn't hate you experienced in my arms a short while ago.'

'I can't stop you possessing my body,' she offered quietly. 'But my mind is entirely my own.'

'And you can't conceive a time when they might both be in accord?'

'Never!'

The edges of his mouth twisted into a cynical smile. 'We shall see.'

She swallowed the sudden lump that rose in her throat, and bravado alone was responsible for the words that left her lips. 'If you've finished with me, I'd like to get up. I need a shower.'

His eyes narrowed in sudden anger, and for a moment she thought he meant to exact retribution, then with a careless shrug he released her, allowing her to slide from the bed where she caught hold of the first thing that came to hand to cover herself before making for the adjoining bathroom.

There, she turned on the water and slipped beneath its cascading, cleansing warmth, and she soaped herself liberally in an effort to be rid of any reminder of Ryan's body.

Dear God! Her limbs began to shake at the thought of what had transpired and her reaction to his lovemaking. Every nerve-end seemed to pulsate in a resurgence of erotic ecstasy, and she relentlessly scrubbed every square inch of her flesh before closing off the water.

He was a brute—an unfeeling, callous *barbarian*! He had successfully ensured that she was chained to him for as long as Michelle was dependent. A horrifying thought suddenly struck—what if there were more children? She would be irretrievably chained for more years than she cared to contemplate. Condemned to a life she couldn't condone with a man she could only hate, subjected to the bittersweet torment of physical lust that was at total variance with her tender emotions. She wanted to scream and rage against fate for being so cruel.

With hurried movements she completed her toilette and slipped into a cool sleeveless cotton dress, tugged a brush through the length of her hair, then crossed the hall to where Michelle had spent the night.

The little girl's bedroom was bathed with early morning sunlight, and Natalie's eyes flew to the far side of the room where Michelle could be seen indulging in what she obviously regarded to be a highly amusing game with her father.

'Martha has already given her a glass of milk,' Ryan informed her calmly, sitting back on his heels. 'Breakfast will be ready in half an hour.'

Michelle sent Natalie a beatific smile across the room, then turned her attention back to Ryan. 'Daddy, Mummy—play!'

For a child whose vocabulary hadn't included 'Daddy' until yesterday, she was adjusting extremely well, Natalie conceded wryly.

'We're endeavouring to build a castle,' Ryan explained. 'Will you help sort out the blocks?'

It was an invitation she had the power to ignore, and despite the fact that all her maternal instincts screamed for her to snatch Michelle into her arms and run as far from Ryan as her legs would carry her, she hesitated to destroy the little girl's newly-acquired trust in the man who would ultimately play a large part in her life.

'Is it to be a round or square castle?' she queried with a faint smile, and crossed the room to sink gracefully down on to her knees. A box containing wooden blocks of all shapes and sizes lay before them—together with a wide variety of toys Natalie had not seen before. It appeared that upon learning he had a child, Ryan had gone out and ordered largely from the toy department in a city store.

'Square will undoubtedly be less complicated,' Ryan declared, setting down a row of foundation blocks. His eyes met hers across the top of Michelle's head, and there was nothing Natalie could do to prevent the erratic thudding pulse at the base of her throat. The edges of his mouth were slanted to form a humorous smile, and his eyes were warm.

Michelle was enchanted to have two adults at her command, and went into a peal of delicious giggles when Ryan hoisted her high onto his shoulder some twenty minutes later.

'I think this young lady is hungry. I know I am!' His deep throaty chuckle did strange things to Natalie's composure, and the laughing smile her daugher received made her oddly wistful. Three years ago *she* had been the recipient of such open affection, and the knowledge seemed to reopen an old wound.

She didn't want his affection, much less his love. So why was she feeling so—resentful? A tiny mirthless laugh bubbled up in her throat. Dear God, she couldn't be jealous of her own daughter! Such a thought was ludicrous!

Breakfast was a convivial meal, with Michelle behaving beautifully. She fed herself with the minimum of fuss, and virtually accident-free twixt spoon and mouth.

Expecting Ryan to leave for the office, Natalie could hardly contain her surprise when he indicated no such intention, electing instead to spend the day getting better acquainted with his wife and daughter.

'Do you think that's wise?' Natalie found herself asking, and incurred a faint mocking smile by return.

'I employ extremely capable men,' Ryan slanted cynically. 'The business won't founder if I'm absent for a day.'

'That wasn't what I meant, and you know it,' she returned civilly.

'Precisely what do you mean?' There was sardonic amusement in his glance, and she had to restrain herself from hurling the first thing that came to hand.

'You're a novelty,' she explained bluntly, and at the sudden flaring in those golden eyes she lifted a hand and pushed a few stray locks of hair behind her ear. It was an outward sign of nervousness, and it irked her that he was aware of it. 'I think Michelle should get used to you gradually,' she ventured slowly, meeting his gaze unflinchingly. 'Young children are very susceptible individuals, and if you're with her constantly for a few days, then absent for five, she's bound to be confused.' Conviction that she was right added strength to her voice. 'She's too young to understand what "Daddy" means, never having known any man except my father, whom she calls "Poppa".' She eyed him steadily, unsure of his mood, for his expression was deliberately enigmatic. 'She may call you Daddy, but it's merely a word without meaning as yet.' She let her hand encompass the room. 'All this—opulence makes a dramatic change from our more humble surroundings. And her room——' she gestured helplessly. 'It's like being let loose in a toyshop! You may feel you're making up for lost time, but I won't have her spoilt.'

'I have no intention of spoiling her, as you call it,' Ryan drawled. 'As for confusing her, I disagree. The transition itself will prove confusing, but I don't see how my presence over the next few days can add to it.'

'Is child psychology one of your attributes? Along with everything else?'

He appeared to hold his temper in check, yet his voice was dangerously soft as he said, 'Natalie, if you want to fight, I'll oblige. But save it for when we're alone. Your talk of children being susceptible to atmosphere doesn't hold much weight when you give every appearance of defying your own dictum.'

'Forgive me,' she managed with implied sarcasm. 'I'd quite forgotten how inflexible and arrogant you can be when crossed!'

His gaze was startlingly direct. 'My, my,' he drawled quietly, 'you are a scratchy bundle of fur this morning!'

'I'm not in the mood to purr,' she snapped, and a gleam of amusement lit his eyes.

'This morning——'

'Was a mistake,' she intercepted swiftly. 'One that I won't permit to be repeated.'

'Indeed?'

Natalie drained the last of her coffee, then replaced the cup on to its saucer before standing to her feet. 'If you'll excuse me? I need some fresh air.' She didn't bother looking at him, merely scooped Michelle from her chair and walked quickly from the room.

On ascending the spiral staircase to the lower level, she unlatched the door that led out to the pool. At this relatively early hour the full impact of the sun's strength was not in evidence, and she let Michelle down to walk while retaining a firm handclasp, witnessing the little girl's delight as they slowly traversed the pool's surround before moving towards the river at the lower edge of the garden. A large cabin cruiser was moored to the pontoon at the end of the jetty, and Natalie made her way slowly towards it.

'Boat,' Michelle pronounced knowledgeably, adding, 'Daddy's boat.'

Whose else could it be but Ryan's? Natalie pondered wryly. The sureness with which Michelle was accepting each and every one of her father's possessions was slightly daunting.

'Ride in Daddy's boat?'

She glanced down at her daughter's blonde locks and caught the open-eyed wonderment in those guileless eyes raised so solemnly, and slowly shook her head. 'Not today, darling.'

'Why?'

'Because, my sweet, your daddy's a busy man. He'll take us for a ride another day.' Obviously a diversion was needed to distract the tot's attention, and with practised adroitness Natalie pointed to a large tabby cat sunning itself on the steps leading to the gazebo, adjacent the pool. 'Come and meet Sasha.'

The cat was a familiar sight, and belonged to Martha, who had adopted him as stray several years before, and he lived an idyllic life bathed in affection, with the run of the grounds and that of

Martha and Jenkins' living quarters.

It was some further ten minutes before they retraced their steps, and on reaching the glass sliding doors Natalie saw Ryan lounging against the aperture. His expression was impossible to discern, and clothed in hip-hugging levis and an open-necked shirt left unbuttoned almost to the waist, he appeared aggressively male and a definite threat to her peace of mind.

'Enjoy your walk?'

To the casual observer his words were an interested query, but Natalie perceived the faint emphasis and substituted 'escape' for 'walk'. He was too perceptive by far, and she longed to retaliate with a sarcastic rejoinder.

'Ride in Daddy's boat,' Michelle demanded with childish candour, and Natalie could only admire her singlemindedness—something that was assuredly inherited from her father!

'Well now,' Ryan drawled, his smile faintly crooked as he slanted a brief enquiring eyebrow towards Natalie before lowering his height with one fluid movement to rest on his haunches, 'I guess we could do that.' His eyes twinkled with warm humour as Michelle viewed him with unblinking solemnity.

'Mummy says Daddy too busy,' the little tot revealed carefully.

'It's a beautiful morning,' Ryan indicated, appearing to give the matter consideration. 'Much too nice to spend indoors. The boat it is, infant.' The corners of his eyes crinkled with laughter as he swept the little girl into the circle of his arm and lifted her high on to his shoulder. 'We'll find Martha and ask her to prepare a picnic lunch.'

Natalie wanted to scream that she didn't want to go—least of all spend the entire day in such close proximity to her indomitable husband. She felt like a puppet, with both Ryan and Michelle manipulating the strings. Yet there was little she could do but appear to give in gracefully. Like it or not, Michelle had the right to become better acquainted with her father, and Ryan was taking steps to ensure that the transition was carried out as smoothly as possible. It was important that there be no apparent dissension if the little girl was to accept their changed circumstances, and much of the success lay with Natalie's attitude. No matter how much she hated to admit it, Ryan was right. Any fights had to be conducted in private— and there would be many!

Weatherwise, it was an idyllic day, with the slightest breeze coming off the Bay to temper the sun's late summer heat. Armed with a bountifully supplied picnic basket, they set off just after ten, Jenkins taking charge behind the wheel as he eased the large cabin cruiser along the Nerang River.

Natalie had taken a similar cruise in those halcyon days just after their marriage, and had been impressed then with the waterways and existing development. Now she viewed the vast changes with interest, especially Paradise Waters and Sorrento, whose blocks bore prestige homes reflecting differing architectural designs. Sparkling swimming pools of various shapes and sizes set in landscaped grounds, the large number of boats and cabin cruisers moored to private jetties, attested to the Coast's affluent society.

Colour abounded in glorious profusion, with the poinciana vying with the bauhinia and the trumpet flower. Clematis and banksia, hibiscus and frangipani provided an exotic background for the splendid stand of tropical palm trees glimpsed in most gardens. Overall, it was a visual paradise, and since it offered such a pleasant climate, little wonder so many people elected to spend and end their days along this coastal strip.

Michelle was more intrigued with the cruiser itself, and Jenkins' handling of it. Between the two men, she was entertained to her delight, and Natalie was inclined to reflect that her own presence was little more than a perfunctory inclusion.

At that precise moment Ryan looked up and caught her gaze, the expression in his tigerish eyes faintly mocking, and she felt a momentary shaft of pain. He was deliberately entrenching himself in Michelle's affections, making any thoughts of a separation untenable. It was almost as if he was forcing her to accept that she could never part them; that he could provide in a way she alone would find impossible. The chains that bound her to Michelle were now forged with steel, and the knowledge that he *knew* rankled unbearably.

Natalie watched in idle fascination as Ryan caught Michelle in his arms and trod with easy, lithe movements to where she stood.

'Feeling neglected?'

She swallowed quickly. 'No. Why should I be?'

He bent forward, lowering his head slightly. 'Liar,' he said softly, and without any warning his lips brushed her temple, then slid down to tease the edge of her mouth before claiming it with a sensuous gentleness that made her ache for more.

The knowledge made her resentful of her own emotions, and her eyes sparked dangerously as she drew back. 'Michelle——'

'Is our daughter,' Ryan interjected sardonically, his eyes agleam with amusement. 'We are responsible for her existence. Eventually she will become aware of it, and all that it implies.'

'She's a little young for a lesson in procreation,' Natalie snapped, and saw a flash of white teeth as he gave a twisted smile.

'Agreed. But evidence of her parents' affection is essential, don't you think?'

Her response was tinged with acrimony. 'You profess to be the expert. Why even consider my opinion?'

The smile didn't reach his eyes, and she felt a shiver of apprehension slither its way from the base of her neck down the length of her spine. 'Behave, Natalie. Otherwise I'll ensure that you regret it.'

'I'm hopelessly outmatched,' she returned lightly, although her eyes were dark and stormy as she met his implacable gaze. 'Perhaps we should stick to the mundane—such as where you intend to stop for lunch, and when.' Her smile was falsely bright. 'Children have an inbuilt clock when it comes to mealtimes!'

Ryan spared the elegantly slim gold watch on his wrist a cursory glance. 'There's a picnic area adjacent the Council grounds at Evandale. We can be there in ten minutes.'

'Excellent,' she concurred with every evidence of charming acceptance. 'I'll take Michelle while you tell Jenkins.'

It was a victory that was really no victory at all, for Michelle's fascination with Ryan meant a few fractious tears when Natalie attempted to retrieve her from her father's arms.

On reflection, it was a pleasant day, despite Natalie's conviction that the hours spent in Ryan's company could only prove disastrous. Jenkins' presence, plus that of Michelle, ensured restraint, and it was something of a relief when the cruiser berthed at the lower edge of the Cronin Island residence in the late afternoon.

Michelle's eyes were drooping as she fought off sleep, and within minutes of entering the house Natalie carried her upstairs, gave her a quick wash, slipped off her outer clothes, then tucked the little girl into bed.

'Have a nice nap, sweetheart,' she bade softly, bending down to bestow a kiss, then with a smile she turned and left the room, closing the door quietly behind her.

The effects of sea-spray and the sun on her skin and hair made her long for a cool refreshing shower, and she crossed the hall, entering the main bedroom to find Ryan in the process of discarding his clothes.

'Oh!' The surprised monosyllable left her lips before she could halt it, and he slanted her a mocking glance.

'We do share a bedroom. Or had you forgotten?'

How could she possibly *forget*? Electing to ignore him, she walked to the capacious wardrobe running the length of one entire wall, slid open a mirrored door and extracted clean underwear. She turned, her eyes widening as she saw Ryan had moved and was standing less than a foot distant. There was a towel slung carelessly about his hips, and the faint male scent of him was flagrantly evocative, stirring her senses so that she was shockingly aware of the sheer animal magnetism he projected.

The hand that reached out and lifted her chin was firm, forcing recognition of his relentless gaze. 'Don't resort to a childish fit of the sulks,' he drawled, and immediately resentment flared.

'I'm not,' she denied, and saw his eyes narrow fractionally.

'No? I find that hard to believe.'

At such proximity he was dangerous—to her peace of mind, and the dictates of her flesh. Already each separate nerve-end tingled alive, craving his touch, and the ache that began deep inside slowly encompassed her body, threatening the slim thread of control she sought so desperately to maintain.

'I'm not used to sharing a room,' she explained, aiming for civility. Nervousness was responsible for the faint parting of her lips, and without conscious thought the edge of her tongue licked slowly along her lower lip. Something flared in those dark golden eyes, and she hastened into speech, the words tumbling forth in an incoherent jumble. 'You startled me—I didn't expect——'

'Michelle has shared your room for more than two years,' Ryan interjected smoothly, letting his gaze rove slowly over her features, noting the heightened colour tinging her cheeks.

'That's—different.'

'It's an incurable addiction, isn't it?' he drawled, making no attempt to free her.

'I don't know what you're talking about,' Natalie responded shakily, and he uttered a soundless derisory laugh.

'Liar! Your body screams for my possession almost as much as mine demands release.'

'Any one would imagine you're the only man who can——'

'Take you to the heights—and beyond?' he finished, cupping her face with both hands, drawing her closer with no effort at all.

'I could have had other lovers,' Natalie voiced the words with contrived conviction, and glimpsed the brief flaring of terrible anger as his eyes searched deep into her very soul, stripping away the protective layers she had spent three years rebuilding with such painstaking care.

'Have you?'

The desire to wound as she had been wounded made her cry out a single monosyllabic affirmative. '*Yes*—damn you! A wild, senseless succession of men only too willing to oblige!'

For a few timeless seconds Ryan looked capable of murder, then his eyes hardened until they resembled topaz chips. 'You have precisely one minute to rescind the reckless folly of those words, and be warned—the truth, this time!'

The seconds pounded with numerical relentlessness through her brain, and as she reached the lower fifties his hold shifted to her shoulders, crushing the delicate bones until she cried out in pain. 'You're hurting me!'

His expression was without mercy, and frighteningly pitiless. At that moment he looked capable of anything, and the words left her lips in a tortured gasp. 'No! No one.' The agonising pressure eased, but only slightly, and she closed her eyes tightly against the damning well of tears threatening to spill in an ignominious stream down her cheeks. Her mouth was trembling so much she could hardly control it, and of their own volition her hands crept up to cover her face.

Natalie had little recollection how long she remained like that, for she seemed locked in a timeless void, conscious only of a feeling of utter devastation.

Slowly, yet with remarkable ease, her hands were prised loose, then her lips were taken, possessed, in a kiss that was punishingly cruel. Without askance, Ryan's mouth forced hers apart, invading its sweetness, plundering, until she could taste the saltiness of her own blood as the soft inner tissue grazed and split against her teeth.

Not content, Ryan sought the zip fastening of her dress, and when it was free, he removed the thin cotton from her body very simply by tearing it to the hem. With deliberate detachment he released the clip of her bra, then tossed it to the carpet. Bare seconds later they were joined by her slip and briefs.

Natalie clutched her arms together in an attempt to cover her breasts, but such effort was soon dashed as he swung her high and carried her to the bed, dropping her unceremoniously down on to its silken coverlet.

He towered over her, large and incredibly menacing, and never had she seen him so consumed with rage. There was controlled violence in the way he looked at her, his eyes raking her nudity with a savage ruthlessness that made her want to shrivel up and die.

'I'm sorry.' The words were scarcely more than a whisper and brought a bitter twist to his mouth.

'You will be, by the time I finish with you!' Hard and implacable, he lowered his body on to the bed beside her, trapping her slimness with his own. His mouth covered hers, insensitive to the pain he was inflicting as he began a ravishment of her senses that sought and punished each sensual pulse and hollow before fastening with devastating intent over the rosy peak of her breast, consuming and alternatively teasing until she uttered a low guttural plea for mercy. Not content, his lips trailed to its twin, his teeth and tongue wreaking havoc until she almost screamed out for him to desist. Like a crazed, demented being she twisted and turned in an effort to escape that torturing mouth, then she gave a whimper of despair as it travelled lower to create a leisurely, ultimate devastation.

She was floating and utterly mindless when Ryan took possession with one single aggressive thrust, and the tiny animal sounds were stilled in her throat as his mouth closed over hers.

Later—although how much later, she was unaware—Ryan carried her into the bathroom, and beneath the warm needle-spray of the shower he soaped and cleansed her body, his touch oddly gentle, before attending to his own needs, then towelled her dry and enveloped her in a silky robe, and with a towel hitched around his hips he dried her hair, brushing it first, then combing it until it flowed like pale silk to her shoulder-blades.

Throughout it all Natalie stood quiescent, her eyes closed against the terrible humiliation and pain she felt deep inside. She wanted to cry, but the tears wouldn't come. At some stage she knew herself to be alone, but she was incapable of moving.

'Drink this.'

It was a command that couldn't be ignored, and when the rim of a glass touched her lips she simply sipped its contents like an obedient child.

The spirits were potent, but palatable, and ran through her veins like warm quicksilver, making her feel strangely weightless.

'Rest for an hour or so,' Ryan instructed brusquely. 'I'll have Martha attend to Michelle. Between us we can feed her and put her to bed.' He lifted a hand and tucked a lock of hair back behind her ear, and without its partially protective curtain Natalie felt exposed and vulnerable. 'We have a dinner engagement,' he told her, his expression inscrutable. 'You remember Rick?'

She did, for he was one of the few of Ryan's

business associates with whom she had felt at ease. A financier based in Melbourne, Rick Andreas had interests in southern Queensland and regularly commuted to the Coast, where he owned a penthouse suite atop one of the more prestigious apartment blocks.

'He married several months ago,' Ryan continued. 'Lisa is anxious to meet you. You'll get on well together.'

Dear lord! *Tonight*? How could she go out and socially shine in company—even if it was only a foursome? Slowly she lifted her eyes to his, seeing little more than a keen intensity in his gaze. 'What time do we leave?' The query was stilted, and she had the strangest feeling someone else had spoken, for the voice didn't seem to be her at all.

A muscle tautened along his jaw, making his features appear harsh and formidable. 'Dammit, Natalie——!' he began explosively.

'Don't worry, Ryan,' she assured him with unaccustomed cynicism, 'I haven't the strength to oppose you.'

'You want an apology for something you deliberately provoked?' he demanded hardily, stifling an oath. 'How the hell did you expect me to react?'

She still felt raw, and an icy numbness seemed to have invaded her bones despite the warm summer heat. 'I can only plead temporary amnesia,' she voiced dully, holding his gaze unwaveringly. 'I should have remembered you possess a wicked temper.'

He remained silent for what seemed an age, and his voice when he spoke was dangerously quiet. 'You have the damnedest ability to arouse a complexity of emotions—some of which are totally unenviable. I'm constantly at odds whether to strangle you or sweep you into wild passionate oblivion.' His eyes were enigmatic as he paused imperceptibly. 'We once shared something beautiful—something that will forever be remembered by Michelle's very existence.'

'That was a long time ago,' Natalie said sadly, suddenly finding it difficult to swallow the lump that had risen to her throat. With a gesture of utter weariness she lifted a hand and massaged her temple in an attempt to ease the dull throbbing there. 'If you don't mind, I'd like to be alone for a while.'

His eyes kindled with a mixture of anger and regret, then became hooded as he turned towards the wardrobe, selecting briefs, immaculate tan trousers and a beige silk shirt. 'I'll ensure you're not disturbed until six. We're meeting Rick and Lisa in the bar of the Lotus Inn at seven.'

CHAPTER SIX

THE restaurant was crowded, and at first glance all the tables appeared to be taken. The smiling waitress was most profuse with her apologies, her manner deferential as she referred to the patrons hugging the bar. 'Mr Andreas is already seated at the table, Mr Marshall. He suggests we serve your drinks there.'

Ryan gave an affirmative nod, and with his arm creating a protective arc about Natalie's waist, he moved aside to follow in the Chinese girl's wake.

Natalie drew a deep steadying breath and uttered a silent prayer for divine assistance to get her through the ensuing few hours. Outwardly she gave the appearance of being a well-dressed socialite; the silky emerald-coloured dress with its swathed bodice and softly-gathered skirt accentuated her slim curves and was a perfect complement to her lightly-tanned skin and striking blonde hair.

Beside her, Ryan was every inch the dominant, successful male. Immaculately groomed in dark hip-hugging trousers and a cream silk shirt left unbuttoned at the neck, he wore the mantle of sophistication with ease. There was a hint of leashed power beneath his rugged exterior, an elusive aura that went with extreme wealth, adding to a whole that would always draw attention— unwanted or not.

'Natalie—Ryan,' a deep voice murmured, its intonation bearing a slight, almost imperceptible accent, and Natalie forced a warm smile as she greeted the tall dark-haired man who had risen to his feet.

'Hello, Rick,' she managed with sincerity. 'It's good to see you again.'

'And you,' he responded quietly, then turning to the young woman seated on his right he gave a slow eloquent smile. 'This is Lisa, my wife.'

Natalie experienced a shaft of envy at his depth of regard for the slim dark-haired girl whose serene features were brought alive by a pair of sparkling dark eyes.

'I'm pleased to meet the woman responsible for Ryan's downfall,' Lisa began, sparing Ryan a twinkling glance. 'I hope we can be friends, Natalie.'

'Thank you—I'd like that.' Natalie took the seat Ryan held out for her, and accepted the slim fluted glass of wine Rick placed on the table before her. It was a light palatable Riesling, and provided a much-needed boost to her sadly low morale.

'It's a little crowded,' Rick remarked, allowing his gaze to encompass the room and its occupants. 'But the food more than compensates.' His eyes were oddly thoughtful as they rested on Natalie. 'I hope this evening will be the first of many we can enjoy together.'

'It will be,' Ryan said smoothly, and he reached out a hand and trailed his fingers down the length of Natalie's arm, then interlaced his fingers with hers. His glance was warm and his smile gentle, and to any onlooker he appeared an adoring husband. 'Natalie and I plan on having a week to ourselves before beginning the inevitable round of entertaining.' He gave a slight shrug and offered a slow teasing smile. 'If the going proves too heavy, I may load up the cruiser and take her off to some remote tropic isle for a while.'

Nick's white teeth flashed in a wicked grin. 'I know just the place. In fact, I own it.' His eyes twinkled with devilish humour as he raised his glass in a silent mocking toast. 'It's yours to use any time you require it.'

Natalie controlled a telling tide of colour which threatened to tinge her cheeks, and threw him a faintly cynical glance. 'You haven't changed, Rick.'

'Ah, but I have,' he declared with a quizzical smile, and Lisa broke in with a musical laugh.

'There's nothing worse than a reformed rake!'

'Alas, I have been tamed. The once-proud lion now permits himself to be led on a chain he has no intention of breaking.' Ryan's eyes held amusement as he spared Lisa a faintly mocking glance, and in an oddly touching gesture he picked up her hand and carried it to his lips.

'You'll have Natalie think I crack a proverbial whip!' his wife protested. 'When, in fact, it was the opposite.'

'Indeed,' he concurred quietly, and Ryan interjected with customary smoothness.

'Shall we order?'

The next few hours passed with reasonable swiftness, the conversational flow maintained with practised ease, so that there was little chance for Natalie to indulge in introspection.

They had been served with a variety of dishes, each kept at an even temperature atop individual silver burners, and replaced at regular intervals with a further selection.

'Dessert?'

'I couldn't,' Natalie refused, more than replete, and Rick cast Lisa a quizzical glance.

'I shouldn't, but I'll have a banana fritter with cream,' his wife decided with a rueful grin. 'I've developed a sweet tooth.'

'Need I enquire why?' Ryan teased, his eyes ablaze with silent laughter, and Lisa picked up her napkin and threatened to throw it at him.

'Wretch!' she laughed. 'I imagine in another month it will be perfectly obvious.'

'I shall be a doting uncle,' he assured her, lifting his glass in a silent salute. 'I couldn't be more happy for you both.'

Lisa turned towards Natalie. 'You have a daughter.' Her eyes became faintly wistful. 'I'd love a little girl. Not that I mind, either way, as long as it comes into the world healthy.' She spared her husband a soft look. 'Rick, like most men, would prefer a son. But a little girl,' she trailed off with a sigh. 'Think of all the pretty clothes, and the fun involved in dressing her!'

'I'm sure I can manage to provide you with both, given time,' her husband declared. 'Meanwhile, you'll have to be patient and see what fate has decreed to send us.' He leaned sideways and bestowed a lingering kiss to her temple. 'I'm going to beg Natalie for a dance while you eat your dessert.'

What else could Natalie do but accept? To refuse would seem churlish, and Rick was too much a friend to offend.

The dance floor was small, the artist and his music a shade too loud, and it was so long since she had danced that at first she stumbled and lost her step.

'Don't apologise,' Rick murmured, pulling her closer to ensure better guidance.

'You're being kind,' she acknowledged with a rueful smile, and incurred his penetrating glance.

'May I say that it's good to see you and Ryan together again?'

Are we? she queried silently. We live in the same

house, share the same table—even the same bed. Yet we couldn't be more apart than if a thousand miles separated us.

'Have I offended you?'

She came out of her reverie and flashed him a bright humourless smile. 'No, of course not.' Heaven help her, she would have to summon forth every reserve of strength. 'You'll have to forgive me, Rick' she began quietly. 'I developed a shocking headache just before we left, and the pills I took have had a rather numbing effect.' The smile reached her eyes as she added sincerely, 'Allow me to congratulate you. Lisa is a lovely girl.'

Rick wasn't fooled, and she knew it, but innate good manners prevented him from probing, and for this she was supremely thankful.

'She's my life,' he revealed softly, and Natalie was unable to prevent the faint prick of tears at the depth of emotion in his voice.

They circled the floor in silence, and when the music paused Rick led her back to their table.

The expression in Ryan's eyes was impossible to discern, and she deliberately avoided his glance, turning instead to Lisa and offering a faint laugh.

'I'm sadly out of practice, I'm afraid. If Rick has sore toes tomorrow, you'll know the reason why!'

'Is that an indirect accusation, darling?' Ryan drawled, and she cast him a sweet smile.

'How could it be?' she countered evenly, lifting her partly-filled glass and savouring the excellent wine. She met his eyes over the rim and wrinkled her nose. 'Although I'd rather it were your toes, and not Rick's, that have to suffer.' The barb was there, but accompanied with a laugh she doubted Rick or Lisa realised its intention.

'In that case, I'd better remedy any remission without delay,' Ryan slanted mockingly, and draining his glass he stood to his feet in one fluid movement.

Natalie could have screamed at her own folly in taunting him. She didn't want to dance, and especially not with her indomitable husband. Yet to refuse would undoubtedly gain an attention she had at all costs to avoid. With the best grace she could muster she allowed him to lead her towards the dance floor, and as his arms closed around her she strained against the inevitable body contact.

'For God's sake, relax,' Ryan bade with accustomed bluntness.

'You have to be joking,' she retaliated swiftly, hating the way he effortlessly moulded her body close to his. 'Do you have to act so convincingly proprietorial?' she demanded seconds later as she felt his fingers trail a tantalising exploratory path over the length of her back.

'Am I?' he demanded lazily, and she felt his lips brush her temple. 'I'm merely following my instincts.'

'And we know what they are!' she retorted, and heard his faint throaty laugh.

'What a little vixen you are, Natalie! You tease, then run, and scream when you're caught.' He slanted her a sardonic twisted smile. 'You're a chameleon, reverting from child to woman and back again at the slightest provocation.'

'And you're totally insufferable!' she hissed, attempting to wriggle out of his grasp. Being so close to him like this made her aware of his muscular hardness, and already his potent magnetism drew her to him like a moth to flame. Every nerve-end quivered vibrantly alive, and she shook her head in a gesture of utter despair. 'I hate you,' she whispered in vengeful avowal. 'I never imagined myself capable of hating anyone as much as I hate you!'

'Stop it,' Ryan warned. 'You've already suffered one painful lesson. Don't give me reason to give you another.'

'And you would,' she retorted bitterly. 'I have to be made to conform—whatever the cost!'

'I'd prefer to conduct our wrangling without a public audience,' he evinced hardily. 'But continue any further and I'm liable to do something regrettable.'

'In a room full of people, your scope is limited,' she retorted with a touch of truculence, and caught the flare of anger that hardened his eyes.

She didn't have time to cry out as his mouth closed over hers in a kiss that was leisurely enough, and as shattering to her equilibrium as he intended.

When he lifted his head she had to cling on to him so that she didn't fall, and seconds later she turned her head into his shoulder in an attempt to hide her humilation.

The music increased in volume and tempo, but Ryan kept to the outer fringe of the floor, his head bent low so that his cheek brushed hers, and to any observers they must have appeared totally engrossed in each other.

It seemed an age before he disentangled his arms and led her back to the table. Her emotions were numbed, and she felt as listless as a rag doll. If Rick or Lisa noticed they had the good sense not to comment, and by mutual consent they ordered coffee, then chose to leave almost immediately.

'I'll ring you,' Lisa declared gently as they reached the street. 'We'll meet for lunch.'

Natalie murmured an appropriate rejoinder,

then, conscious of Ryan's firm grasp at her elbow, she bade them both goodnight and allowed him to lead her towards the car.

Seated inside its luxurious interior, she went through the motions of fastening her seatbelt with the movements of an automaton, dimly aware that he had slipped in behind the wheel and was intent on manoeuvring the large vehicle into the stream of traffic.

Wearily she leaned her head back against the headrest and closed her eyes. She felt an emotional wreck, and so physically tired she was ill-equipped to face the inevitable recriminations that would follow once they reached home.

It took five minutes to gain access to the small bridge that led to Cronin Island, and a further minute for the car to sweep through the remote-controlled gates and halt inside the garage.

Without a word she slid out of her seat and followed him into the house, crossing the large entrance foyer to the stairs, mounting each step with an odd sense of fatalism as they led her ever nearer to the upper floor and ultimately to their bedroom.

The decisive click of the door as it closed behind her had a strange effect on her nerves, making them jangle in painful discord, and she turned to face him in an oddly defensive movement.

In the shadowed half-light from a distant bedlamp Ryan appeared large and formidable, his stance vaguely menacing as he moved towards her.

Suddenly Natalie didn't care any more, and she closed her eyes in an attempt to shut out the sight of him. Maybe if she prayed very hard, when she opened her eyes it would be to discover all this was part of a nightmare. Silly, stupid tears welled up behind her lids and seeped through to trickle slowly down each cheek until they came to rest at the edge of her chin.

She sensed rather than heard him move, and felt the featherlight brush of his fingers as they trailed the path of her tears.

'You sweet fool,' Ryan muttered with wry gentleness, and tilting her chin he slid a hand beneath the heavy swathe of her hair to hold fast her head, then his lips touched each closed eyelid in turn before slipping to her temple and teasing a downward path to the softly-beating pulse at the base of her neck.

Slowly and with infinite care he removed her dress, and she shivered as her slip, then her bra and briefs fell to the floor.

A barely-stifled oath left Ryan's lips as he saw the faint bruising evident on her delicate skin, and she swayed beneath his touch as he brushed his lips to each painful bruise in turn.

Despite a despondent lethargy her traitorous body began to respond, and she groaned in despair. 'Don't—please!' Her voice trailed off in an aching sob. 'I couldn't bear any more.'

His mouth covered hers, his tongue teasing an evocative path along her lower lip. 'I'm going to put you to bed,' he murmured, his warm breath invading her mouth.

'But not alone,' she said sadly, unable to open her eyes, and she felt his lips twist beneath hers.

'Do you want to be alone?'

She started to nod, then gave a slow shake of her head. 'I want to sleep.' A convulsive sob choked in her throat. What was the use of begging? He was immune to any plea she might make.

In a single movement he lifted her into his arms and carried her to the large bed, then lowered her between the sheets. She could hear the faint rustle of clothing, then the edge of the bed depressed as he slid in beside her, and in the darkness he reached out, drawing her close and cradling her into the curve of his body. As a hand covered her breast she stiffened, then as he made no attempt to caress she gradually relaxed, her breathing steadying until its even rise and fall revealed a slip into blissful somnolent oblivion.

The following few days were a delight, for with Ryan absent from eight in the morning until six at night, Natalie was able to devote the daylight hours to Michelle. Together they swam in the pool, explored the garden and grounds, then with Jenkins' escort—at Ryan's insistence—the little girl was introduced to the first of the Coast's entertainment facilities. With such a variety, it was difficult to choose, but Sea World won the day, and Michelle was entranced with the performing dolphins, the sea-lions and tiny penguins.

'More, more!' she demanded when it was time to leave, and Natalie declared firmly that they would come another day. It would prove all too easy to indulge her. As it was, being Ryan's daughter, she would soon grow accustomed to luxury and the material possessions that wealth could provide. It was essential to establish and maintain an even balance, especially as Michelle was a very perceptive child and able to distinguish a difference between her former and her present lifestyle.

Without Ryan's disturbing presence Natalie was able to relax, although the evenings were something she preferred not to give much thought to. She came to anticipate the time he was due to return, unconsciously listening for the sound of the car in the driveway, the closing of a door followed by his entrance into the house. Together with Michelle, who had been fed an hour before, she would wait for him in the lounge. There they would share a drink while Ryan questioned them about their day, and the increasing rapport between father and daughter was something Natalie could only reluctantly admire, even though it hurt unbearably that the little girl's affections could be so easily won. At seven, amidst giggles and delighted shrieks of laughter, Michelle was lifted high on to her father's shoulders and carried upstairs to bed, where, with predictable delaying tactics, she managed to extend her bedtime for a further fifteen minutes as she alternately begged a drink or stressed the necessity for another visit to the bathroom.

Dinner was served at seven-thirty, and after settling Michelle, Ryan would shower and change his clothes, then escort Natalie down to the dining room. This was the time she came to dread, for inevitably before the main course was halfway through he had managed to put her on the defensive, making it almost impossible for her to maintain civility. By the time coffee was served, they were engrossed in verbal battle—not that she was any match for his brand of sardonic cynicism.

On Thursday evening, exactly a week from the day she had returned to Ryan's household, he emerged from the shower and entered the bedroom with lithe easy movements, his tall frame bare apart from the towel hitched casually about his hips.

'Change into something more sophisticated,' he ordered without preamble. 'We're dining out.' He crossed to the wardrobe, and Natalie watched in idle fascination as he extracted dark trousers and a dark silk-print shirt, then began the process of dressing.

'Where?' she queried, and instantly incurred a dark slanting glance.

'Does it matter?'

'I don't possess anything terribly sophisticated,' she responded evenly, meeting his gaze. 'Fashions have changed over the past three years, and I haven't been able to afford to compete with the latest trend.'

One eyebrow rose in quizzical mockery. 'You mean you haven't already indulged in a madly expensive spending spree?'

'I left all those plastic credit cards behind, if you remember?' she countered sweetly, and his eyes narrowed with an angry gleam.

'Why the hell didn't you ask? Jenkins has instructions to give you any money you might need.'

'Oh, Jenkins has been discretion itself,' Natalie declared in swift defence. 'However, I could hardly ask him for an advance on my clothing allowance.'

'You could have asked me.'

She flicked a stray lock of hair back behind her ear, and met his gaze fearlessly. 'I once begged you to give me financial assistance to help my father, and you refused. I'll never put myself in the invidious position of having to ask anything of you again!'

His answering silence held an element of danger, and she involuntarily tensed, unconsciously holding her breath as he subjected her to a long analytical appraisal before saying in a quiet voice that sent icy shivers slithering down her spine, 'That particular request rapidly transgressed into a verbal battle.' His eyes resembled hard topaz chips that speared her mercilessly. 'I was in no mood to grant your request.'

'Perhaps I should have been more forthcoming

and offered my body,' Natalie heard the words slip from her lips before she had given them conscious thought.

Ryan gave every appearance of keeping a tight rein on his temper. 'I'll forget you said that.'

She closed her eyes momentarily, then turned away with a gesture of weariness. 'I'll get changed,' she said quietly. Fighting him could only lead to destruction—hers. Perhaps it was better to concede defeat before he gained an invaluable foothold on her emotions. Heaven knew it was difficult enough to cope with each physical onslaught without providing additional provocation. Yet subconsciously some tiny imp seemed to urge her into fresh battle at almost every turn, and it galled her unbearably that he continually triumphed.

Crossing to her wardrobe, she selected a slim-skirted black sleeveless dress with a draped bodice whose neckline was anything but demure, plunging as it did almost to her waist at the back and front. Slim high-heeled black sandals gave her added height, and she fastened a silver locket that had belonged to her grandmother around her neck, then attended to her make-up before brushing her hair so that it swung loose about her shoulders. A light spray of perfume to several pulse-spots, and she collected an evening purse from a drawer, slipped in lipstick, comb, powder compact and a handkerchief, then turned towards the door.

'I'm ready.'

Ryan stood seemingly relaxed and at ease, his eyes hooded, making his expression difficult to discern. He opened the door and stood aside, following as she walked down the hall to the stairs.

Jenkins had already brought the car around, and he bade them goodnight as they left the house.

It was warm outside after the air-conditioned interior of the house, and Natalie slid into the passenger seat of the waiting Ferrari, reached for the safety-belt and fastened it as Ryan slipped in behind the wheel.

'Where are we going?'

The powerful car had negotiated the Chevron bridge and was purring with leashed ease past the golf course, heading west towards the hills.

'Nerang.'

'Good heavens,' she exclaimed. 'You are informative!'

His eyes didn't shift from the road. 'There's an old renovated homestead that has been converted into a restaurant,' he explained with seeming patience. 'The food is excellent, and the atmosphere quiet and intimate. It's a little different from the usual, and I think you'll enjoy it.'

The dusk of evening had disappeared and the car's powerful headlights picked out the surrounding bush-clad terrain, which in turn gave way to housing developments.

Natalie took in the changes with interest. The last time she had passed along this particular road there was scarcely a house to be seen. Now there were factories and houses at irregular intervals, giving credence to the Coast's industrial growth over the past few years.

'Are we dining alone?' She voiced the query idly, more as something to say than a desire for knowledge.

'Yes.'

'Oh.'

Ryan spared her a swift glance. 'Such enthusiasm,' he mocked sardonically. 'Do you find my sole company so daunting?'

She swallowed quickly and gave a slight shrug. 'Whenever we're alone, we usually quarrel.'

'I'm sure we'll manage to maintain a modicum of civility,' he drawled. 'There'll be others present. The place is well patronised.'

Natalie retreated into silence as he brought the car to a smooth halt at a busy intersection. After gaining a pause in the traffic he swung the wheel with smooth efficiency and eased into a parking space.

Switching off the ignition, he reached into the rear compartment and withdrew two bottles. 'It isn't licensed, so we bring our own,' he explained with an edge of mockery, and she slid out to walk at his side towards the nondescript cottage, whose only claim to being an exclusive eatery was its sparkling neon sign.

The contrast inside was dramatic. Dark-stained timbered walls and ceilings, soft lighting, heavy lace curtaining masking the windows, all lent an olde-wordle atmosphere. Immaculate white linen and gleaming silverware created an elegance that was matched by the attentive staff.

Their table was tucked away in a quiet corner, and Natalie took a sip of excellent German Riesling as she perused the blackboard menu.

'Any particular preference?'

She glanced towards that drawling voice and tried to ignore the way her senses leapt at the mere sight of him. It was crazy how she could alternate between dislike and its antithesis with such rapidity. 'Mmn,' she deliberated, scanning the dishes offered. 'I'll have fish, I think, barramundi meuniere, with no starter.'

'My appetite is a little more substantial than yours,' said Ryan, giving her order. 'I'll start with peppered prawns, and have scallopini with mushrooms to follow. Vegetables, no salad. Natalie?'

'Oh, salad, thank you.'

His faint amusing gleam put her slightly on the defensive.

'I happen to like salad.'

'Did I suggest that you didn't?'

'I've come a long way since the days when I followed your every lead,' she said lightly, taking the sting out of her words with a slight smile.

The waitress arrived with a small wooden board containing a crusty loaf and a pot of garlic butter, which she placed beside Ryan.

He lifted the serrated knife and proceeded to cut it into slices, which he buttered, then placed one on to Natalie's plate.

'I could have done that,' she protested, accepting the slice, and promptly bit into it, finding it delicious.

'Indulge me. I'm in an attentive mood.'

'My goodness!' She allowed her eyes to widen deliberately. 'This moment will have to be recorded for posterity.'

'Drink your wine,' he drawled, refilling her glass, and she wrinkled her nose at him.

'I know your game. You're trying to lull me into a warm dreamy state, so that I won't have the inclination to argue.'

He lifted his glass and touched its rim to hers, his eyes faintly mocking. 'Here's to us.'

'I'm not sure I should drink to that.'

'Why ever not?'

'It might lead to my downfall.'

'Would that be so very bad?' he queried with unaccustomed gentleness, and she nodded.

'Oh yes,' she said sadly. 'I fell in love with you once. It was like being enclosed in a beautiful bubble, flying higher and higher with the rays of the sun shooting its translucent film with a myriad pretty colours. I thought I was immune from the rest of the world, protected, and infinitely precious.' She met his gaze unflinchingly. 'One day the bubble burst, and I crashed painfully down to earth.' She lifted her glass and stared at its contents. 'It isn't an experience I want to repeat.'

'Fate is an incredible entity,' Ryan began after a measurable silence, and anything further he might have said was lost by the presence of the waitress as she deposited a dish of peppered prawns before him.

The aroma tantalised her nostrils, activating her taste-buds, and as he lifted the first prawn to his mouth he caught her faintly wistful expression.

'Like to try one?'

She watched as he replaced the fork into the dish, and when he lifted a succulent morsel and fed it into her mouth she didn't refuse. With a strange fascination she accepted two more mouthfuls, aware of the blatant sensuality in sharing his food and the same utensil. It was almost as if he was deliberately attempting to establish that they shared something more tangible than mere food, and the knowledge was so profound she didn't dare dwell on it.

'You're treating me like a child,' she breathed shakily, and was unable to glance away from the depth of his probing gaze.

'Am I?' There was no mockery evident, and for a moment she was totally oblivious to everyone else in the room.

With a sense of mounting panic she reached for her glass and resolutely sipped its contents. Dear God, what was the matter with her? The wine, the food, Ryan's manner, all seemed part of a flagrant seduction. She had only to close her eyes and the past three years might never have been.

'Have another slice of bread.'

Natalie regarded the proffered board, and shook her head. It was perhaps as well that at that precise moment the waitress returned to clear Ryan's dish and set their main course before them.

The barramundi fillet melted in her mouth, and the delicate sauce was a perfect complement.

'Dessert?'

Natalie shook her head and finished the last of her wine. 'No. Thank you.'

'Irish coffee? Or perhaps a Royale?' Ryan suggested, leaning well back in his chair. 'An excellent way to finish off a meal, don't you agree?'

Rich black coffee spiced with spirits and topped with cream had a definite appeal, and she nodded in silent acquiescence.

With calm unhurried movements he extracted cigarettes and a lighter, then when the slim tube was lit to his satisfaction he exhaled the smoke with every evidence of pleasure.

'It's only ten. Would you like to take in a show after we leave here?'

The thought of crowds of people, bright glaring lights and noise after these peaceful surroundings prompted her to refuse. 'Besides, you have work tomorrow,' she added, sipping the delicious hot coffee from its pottery goblet. She felt sated with good food and wine, relaxed, and vaguely sleepy.

'I'm taking the day off,' Ryan informed her blandly, and through a haze of smoke his expression was difficult to discern.

She managed a slight smile. 'Any particular reason?'

'A shopping excursion—yours and Michelle's.'

'We're to be suitably fitted out in a style accustomed to your standing,' she declared evenly. 'May I point out that Michelle will become tired and fractious after an hour or two?'

'I hadn't bargained on bringing her along. Martha is quite capable of looking after her.'

'I didn't realise my clothes were so sadly lacking.'

'Your clothes are fine,' Ryan asserted, his dark golden eyes giving evidence of an appreciative appraisal as they swept down the deep vee of her bodice. 'You simply need more. We're having a few people in for dinner on Saturday evening.'

Natalie felt her heart sink, and she finished the rest of her coffee before flashing him a brilliant smile. 'In that case a shopping spree is definitely in order. It will be very important that I shine and dazzle effectively, and for that I must dress the part.'

'Shall we go?'

His hand was firm on the back of her waist as they threaded their way to the front desk, and outside he saw her seated in the car before crossing round to slip in behind the wheel.

The drive home was accomplished in what seemed a very short time. Why was it that the return journey always appeared to be *less*? Natalie mused as she followed Ryan into the house.

She crossed the carpet to the stairs, and paused to slip off her sandals before ascending to the upper floor with the straps dangling from her fingers. In the bedroom she switched on the light and moved to the bathroom, cleansed her skin of make-up, brushed her teeth, then retraced her steps.

Ryan was standing near the window, the scene beyond the partially curtained glass apparently holding his attention. One hand was thrust into his trouser pocket, and in the dim glow cast from a solitary bedlamp he appeared to tower even taller than his six feet three inches.

Natalie extracted a filmy nightgown from beneath her pillow and donned it after shedding her clothes, then she crossed to the mirrored dresser and picked up her brush.

She was halfway through the customary number of strokes when the brush was taken from her hand, and she gave Ryan's shadowy reflection a startled glance as he began to stroke the brush through the length of her hair.

'It's like pale spun silk,' he murmured, letting it slip slowly through his fingers as if the feel fascinated him.

There was an odd familiarity in his touch that brought a return of the past, and Natalie closed her eyes in an effort to dispel the memory it evoked. As if encased in a magical hypnotic spell she sat quiescent as he lifted a swathe of hair and gently brushed his lips against her nape. She was powerless to move away, or even speak, and as his mouth trailed to a vulnerable hollow at the base of her throat she gave an inaudible moan, aware of the slow pulsing ache that threatened her treacherous emotions, yet she was powerless to stop their response.

In a dreamlike trance she felt him lift and turn her so that she stood resting against his hard lean frame, and as his mouth closed over hers she let her arms slowly encircle his neck.

His mouth created its own havoc, filling her senses with bittersweet warmth until she clung to him like a wild untamed creature craving fulfilment. Nothing else mattered but the satisfaction of his possession, and like a priceless musical instrument he played her emotions to their fullest extent before staking his claim in an action that soared them both high to a plateau of mutual ecstasy.

CHAPTER SEVEN

RYAN was as good as his word, and early next morning they drove into Surfer's Paradise, where, within a very short space of time, the back seat and the boot of the Daimler were filled with a variety of boxes in all shapes and sizes.

Natalie's head spun at the speed with which it was all accomplished, and when Ryan suggested a drink, she allowed him to lead her into a small but select coffee lounge.

'Hmn, I needed that,' she murmured appreciatively as she sipped a superbly-brewed cappuccino. Her eyes were drawn to his, and she was unable to prevent the query, 'Who have you invited to dinner tomorrow night?'

His eyes gleamed with hidden mockery. 'Scared?'

She grimaced slightly. 'Apprehensive. I doubt I'll ever make a serene hostess.'

'There aren't many around,' he allowed cynically. 'It's all a clever façade. Inside, they're desperately afraid, and only practice and maturity brings a semblance of serenity.'

'So,' she declared ruefully. 'Forewarned is forearmed. Are Rick and Lisa coming?'

'They are, together with the Richardsons, a few business associates and their partners.'

'Not Simone?' The words were out before she could stop them, and it took considerable courage to hold his gaze.

'Not to my knowledge,' Ryan responded evenly. 'However, it's possible she could partner either of two associates.' His eyes narrowed slightly until they resembled topaz chips. 'I don't doubt you can handle it if she does turn up.'

'Oh, I'm sure she will,' she said with a brittle smile. 'Turn up, I mean. In fact, I wouldn't put it past her to deliberately manipulate the invitation.'

Throughout the next day Natalie was a mass of nerves, and she showered and changed into one of her new dresses—a soft synthetic material in subtle shades of pink, lilac and grey that highlighted her blonde hair and glowing skin. Her make-up was applied with time-consuming care, and a liberal spray of Miss Dior to several pulse-beats added the finishing touch.

'Very pleasing,' Ryan drawled as he entered the bedroom from the bathroom, and she inclined her head in a mocking acceptance of his compliment.

'Thank you, kind sir.' She let her eyes wander over his dark trousers and immaculate pale shirt. 'You, too, will pass muster.'

One eyebrow slanted in cynical appraisal. 'I think you could do with a drink. Shall we go downstairs?'

'Into battle,' Natalie inclined impishly, and allowed him to take her elbow.

It was amazing what a glass of wine could do to boost her morale, she mused some fifteen minutes later, and when Jenkins escorted Nick and Lisa Andreas into the lounge she went forward to greet them with genuine warmth.

Within the space of ten minutes all but two of their guests had arrived, and Natalie felt the tension knot in her stomach as Jenkins ushered in a tall dark-haired man whose face appeared vaguely familiar, and the knot tightened when she saw his companion.

Simone Vesey was sophistication personified,

from the top of her elegantly-coiffured dark head
to the tip of her imported shoes. Attired in black,
her make-up superb, she drew the attention of
every pair of eyes in the room.

Good manners alone carried Natalie through
the ensuing ten minutes, and afterwards she could
not have recounted a word as she smiled and
exchanged polite small-talk with their guests.

It was a relief when dinner was announced, and
throughout the numerous courses she strived to
act out a part in which she felt totally ill at ease,
and it was mostly due to Lisa and Rick Andreas,
seated close by, that her attention was averted
from Simone's blatant attempt to flirt with Ryan.

To give him his due, he didn't respond, but it
rankled nonetheless, and Natalie felt her eyes
being drawn more and more often towards them.

How she managed to get through the remainder
of the evening was a mystery, although the
assistance of several glasses of wine no doubt
helped! The room, the guests—all seemed cloaked
with a sense of *déjà vu*, and brought back a vivid
recollection of several evenings in the past when
she and Ryan had entertained guests, several of
whom were present tonight.

After coffee had been served in the lounge, one
couple then another began to disperse, until only
Simone and Gordon White remained.

'Darling, I must congratulate you on effecting a
reconcilation with Ryan,' smiled Simone with
superficial civility, but there was only enmity
evident in those brilliant dark eyes as she fixed
Natalie with a raking stare.

'Thank you,' Natalie managed evenly, aware
that Ryan and Gordon were deep in conversation
and therefore partly oblivious to what was taking
part between Simone and herself.

'I'm sure you worked very hard.'

Natalie gave a polite smile. 'If you choose to think so.'

A thin stream of smoke rose from the slender cigarette Simone held, and she lifted it to her mouth, took a long inhalation, then expelled the smoke with every evidence of satisfaction. 'He was on the point of instigating divorce before you hit him with your—er—*pièce de résistance*, shall we say? So convincing to be able to produce a child.' Her eyes glittered angrily. 'It's to be hoped Ryan took the precaution of checking the blood grouping. Subtler tricks than yours have been worked in the past, and he is a very wealthy man.'

'You haven't changed, Simone,' Natalie remarked wryly.

'No, darling—and I never will,' the dark-haired woman breathed with thinly disguised emnity.

Natalie caught Ryan's narrowed glance and offered him a brilliant smile, then crossed to his side. 'Simone was just saying they must leave.' She let her gaze shift to his companion. 'It's been a pleasure meeting you, Gordon.'

It seemed natural to move towards the door, and she could hardly believe it was all over as she stood at Ryan's side in the foyer and bade them goodnight.

The instant the door closed she turned and made for the stairs. 'I'm going to bed.'

'Nothing more to drink?' Ryan slanted, and she rounded on him with a hollow laugh.

'Are you trying to suggest I've had more than I can handle?'

'Did I say that?' he queried with a bland inscrutability, and anger rose to the fore with a vengeance.

'Oh, go to hell, Ryan! I'm tired, and after

fielding Simone's vicious innuendoes, I'm in no mood to continue with yours!'

'You hardly spoke to her all evening,' he commented with a narrowed glance, and she erupted into angry speech.

'You more than made up for my lapse in that direction!' she spat furiously, and his eyes gleamed with mocking cynicism.

'I do believe you're jealous. Are you?'

'You have to be kidding!'

She watched in idle fascination as he crossed to her side, and his husky laugh was more than she could bear.

'I think you protest too much, my darling wife,' he uttered quizzically, and without thought her hand flew to his face.

'Oh no,' Ryan cautioned softly as he caught it in mid-air, then deftly twisted it behind her back. 'If you want to fight, we'll do it in the privacy of our bedroom. Then there'll be no doubt as to its conclusion.'

'I hate you,' she breathed bitterly. 'My God, you don't know how much!'

Without another word he swung her into his arms and carried her up the stairs, oblivious to the fists she rained against his powerful back, and in their room he threw her on to the bed, then joined her there.

What followed remained indelibly imprinted in her brain, and even as she begged for mercy her traitorous body arched and twisted beneath his, silently urging him towards a tumultuous, raging, almost raping, possession.

She slept deeply, haunted by dreams in which she was a shadowy participant, yet when she woke she retained no recollection of those somnolent sequences. Only Ryan and the events of the previous evening flooded forth with dreadful clarity, and she turned her head cautiously only to see that she was alone in the large bed. A glance at her watch revealed that it was after eight, and she breathed a small sigh of relief that he would already have breakfasted and left for the golf course.

She rose and showered, then dressed and went downstairs to join Michelle for the first meal of the day.

'Swim, Mummy!'

Natalie sipped her coffee and bit into her toast. 'After, sweetheart. It's going to be a lovely warm day. We'll sit out by the pool, and you can draw some pictures while I read the newspaper. Then we'll swim, okay?'

'Yes, please.'

They finished their breakfast, then changed into swimsuits before going downstairs to the pebbled courtyard adjoining the pool. Natalie smoothed some sunscreen cream over the little girl's skin, then rendered a similar treatment to her own.

The time passed swiftly, and after giving Michelle a swimming lesson she stretched out on a canvas chair and let the sun's warmth dry the moisture from her skin.

A slight sound alerted her, and she looked up to see Martha hurrying forward, her pleasant features faintly anxious.

'A long-distance call, Natalie, from Mrs Maclean.'

Natalie stood to her feet in one fluid movement. 'I'll take it on the bar extension,' she declared, her eyes darting to the tiny figure happily engrossed with toys not too far distant from the pool's edge. 'Will you watch Michelle?'

Her feet almost flew across the pebbled

courtyard, and she picked up the receiver with shaky fingers. 'Andrea?'

'I'm at the hospital,' her stepmother declared without preamble. 'They're preparing John for surgery immediately. I'll ring you the minute he comes out.'

'How is he?'

'As fit as he'll ever be to withstand the operation. The light's flashing, Natalie, and I haven't any more coins.'

'I'll catch the next flight down,' Natalie declared, voicing the words even as the intention entered her head, then the line bleeped and went dead. 'Damn!' She replaced the receiver and reached for the telephone directory, finding the number she wanted with the minimum of effort. Dialling the digits, she waited impatiently for the airline to answer. 'Hello? This is an emergency. I want a seat on the first flight to Sydney. I can be at the airport in less than an hour.' She listened attentively, then said a decisive 'Thanks'. God— three-quarters of an hour was cutting it fine! Especially as she hadn't even packed! 'Martha?'

That good woman almost ran in her haste to give assistance, a protesting Michelle scooped against an ample bosom.

'Can you tell Jenkins to get the car ready, then help me pack? We'll have to achieve a minor miracle if I'm to make that flight out of Coolangatta on time!'

'Are you taking Michelle?'

Natalie didn't even pause as she ran towards the stairs. 'Of course. I couldn't leave her behind.'

The next fifteen minutes were a mixture of well-organised confusion and total chaos, but un-believably there were two suitcases stowed in the boot of the powerful Daimler, both she and

Michelle were presentably clothed, and Jenkins was handling the powerful car with skilful efficiency as it sped down the coastal highway.

The jet was actually warming up on the tarmac when they reached the airport, and with Jenkins' help they made it—just, being last to board.

An hour later they landed at Sydney's Mascot airport, and were immediately whisked by taxi to the hospital.

'You brought Michelle?' Andrea queried, faint disapproval creasing her brow. 'Natalie, she would have been better left at home. A hospital isn't the place for young children.'

'I just packed and left without thinking about it,' she answered. 'Any news yet?'

'He's still in surgery. Oh, dear Lord, it's been so long!' Tears welled up behind tired blue eyes, and Natalie felt a surge of compassion for the older woman.

'Hey, he's my father,' she said gently. 'I love him too.'

Andrea nodded in silence. 'He's all I have,' she declared brokenly.

'Shall I get you a cup of coffee? Have you had anything to eat?' Her own stomach felt empty, for she had been too engrossed with feeding Michelle to bother about her own needs. 'You take Michelle while I ask at reception.'

She was back in five minutes carrying a tray on which reposed two steaming cups of coffee and a plate of sandwiches. 'We'll both feel better when we've had this.'

Andrea undid a sachet of sugar and stirred her coffee abstractedly, her eyes darting to the front desk at every sound or movement from that direction.

'Have something to eat,' Natalie cajoled. 'Even

when Dad comes out from theatre, it will be at least an hour or two before the anaesthetic begins to wear off, and even then he'll drift in and out of sleep for several hours. You don't want his first glimpse of you to cause him any concern.'

'Do I look that bad?' Andrea asked ruefully. 'I haven't slept for the past two nights worrying about the outcome of all this.'

'It shows—a little,' Natalie agreed with a slight grin. 'But you're far from appearing haggard. Now, please—eat. For Dad's sake, if not for your own.'

The hours seemed interminable, and keeping Michelle suitably amused proved something of a distraction—a not unwelcome one, for conversation was at a low ebb.

It was almost four o'clock when a gowned, bespectacled man entered the waiting room, and Andrea immediately sprang to her feet wearing an agonisingly anxious expression.

'John—is he all right? Please——'

'Mr Maclean is in the recovery room,' the surgeon soothed with the ease of long practice. 'He'll be taken to his suite in about half an hour. Sister will allow you to see him very briefly, but I must warn you that it will be several hours before he'll regain full consciousness.' His eyes kindled with professional warmth. 'I would advise that you go home, have a meal, then return later this evening.'

'Has the operation been a success?' Andrea's eyes were almost stark with fear, and Natalie held her breath for his reply.

'It's much too early to be conclusive, Mrs Maclean. Several factors have to be considered before I'm prepared to give an assessment. Rest assured he's in the best possible hands.'

It was professional ambiguity at best, and Natalie sensed Andrea's inner anguish at not having her worst fears either confirmed or denied.

'I'll stay with you,' she reassured her, and the older woman nodded her silent appreciation.

'You'd better ring Ryan.'

Ryan? She hadn't even thought to leave a message, although Martha or Jenkins would inform him of her whereabouts. A wry smile tugged the corners of her mouth. This episode would merely be another in a rapidly-growing string of events to be chalked up against her. She seemed to anger him at every turn—as he angered *her*. Whenever they were together the air was fraught with latent animosity. Some devilish imp impelled her to behave in a manner that was totally alien to her nature, delighting in being as deliberately perverse as possible, so that his resultant wrath heaped retribution upon her hapless head.

'I'll ring him this evening from the hotel,' Natalie murmured, delaying the inevitable.

'Where are you staying?' Andrea asked him in an abstracted manner, and Natalie gave a rueful laugh.

'Would you believe—I don't know? I came straight here from the airport.' She picked up the magazine Michelle had dropped and re-opened the pages. 'I'll beg some assistance from the receptionist. Maybe she can recommend a reasonable place. Otherwise, I'll simply pick something at random from the directory.'

'Natalie?'

She turned slightly, waiting, and Andrea said quietly, 'Thank you for coming.'

'It never occurred to me not to,' she responded

gently, then resumed her way to the reception desk.

'Mrs Marshall?'

Natalie nodded in faint puzzlement.

'I have Mr Marshall on the line. Will you take the call from this phone?' She indicated a telephone set at the edge of her desk, and Natalie drew a deep steadying breath as she crossed to pick up the receiver.

'Ryan?'

'I'm at the airport.' His voice was unnecessarily brusque. 'Stay at the hospital until I get there.'

He hung up before she had a chance to say anything, and immediately resentment rose to the fore. Of all the nerve! Calmly ignoring his directive, she set about arranging accommodation for herself and Michelle, then returned to resume her seat beside Andrea.

Almost twenty minutes later an officious-looking Sister entered the waiting-room and summoned Andrea. 'Only a few minutes, Mrs Maclean,' she insisted, sparing Natalie a quick glance. 'Alone, I'm afraid.'

Natalie gave her stepmother an encouraging smile, and watched as both women disappeared from view.

'Hungry, Mummy,' Michelle asserted with childish candour, and Natalie cast a swift glance at the clock on the wall.

'Soon, sweetheart.'

Andrea's features were pale when she returned, and Natalie stood to her feet at once, concern uppermost.

'I'll ring for a taxi. It can drop you at your sister's house, then take us on to the hotel.'

Mercifully, they were able to leave the hospital in a very short space of time, and after depositing

Andrea, Natalie directed the driver to the address in King's Cross.

After checking in to her room, food was the first consideration, and Natalie dialled room service to place an order.

Michelle was irritable and tired, as well as being hungry, and had become almost impossible to manage.

'Darling, don't cry,' she begged, attempting to soothe the little girl. 'Let's go the bathroom and wash, then we'll switch on the television, and before you know it there'll be a knock on the door and our dinner will be here.'

'Daddy!' Michelle wailed, and Natalie moment-arily closed her eyes before crossing to the bathroom.

Within minutes there was a knock on the outer door, and she gave a sigh of relief. Food, at last!

Expecting to see the waiter, she took a few speechless seconds to register Ryan's tall frame as she opened the door.

'What are you doing here?'

Dark slim-fitting trousers and a dark patterned shirt lent him a grim implacable air, and anger emanated beneath the surface of his control. 'I could ask you the same question.'

'Daddy!' Michelle's tiny body hurtled towards them and almost flew into the arms that reached to lift her high against a powerful chest.

At that precise moment the waiter appeared with a covered tray, adding to the general confusion, and it was a few minutes before the door closed after his retreating figure.

'Hungry,' the little girl insisted mournfully, looking from one parent to the other with big reproachful eyes, and Ryan crossed to the table, set his daughter in a chair and proceeded to feed her.

'I can do that,' Natalie protested, eyeing him warily.

'Ring room service and order another meal,' he instructed hardily.

She drew a deep breath, then crossed to the phone. 'What do you want?'

'Anything. I'm not fussy.'

The order placed, she moved to the table and sat down. Suddenly she wasn't hungry any more, and she toyed with the food on her plate, pushing it back and forth like a child confronted with food deemed obnoxious to its palate.

Her hunger sustained, Michelle scrambled down to sit happily on the carpet in front of the television set, oblivious to all but the flickering screen.

'Is this——' Ryan cast a glance at the room before swinging back to fix her with an unwavering glare, 'another act of defiance?'

'You had no need to race after me,' Natalie hissed through clenched teeth. 'I'm quite capable of looking after myself.'

'Did I imply that you weren't?'

'Then why are you here?' she demanded truculently.

'Depending on the outcome of the operation, I thought you might need my support,' he declared dryly, and her eyes moved to a point beyond his right shoulder.

'Such concern,' she mocked lightly, ignoring the angry tensing of his jaw as she met his gaze. 'For a moment I believed you'd come to check that I hadn't absconded with Michelle.'

Hard topaz chips gleamed beneath his partially hooded lids, and her stomach muscles tightened into a painful knot at the anger evident.

'You wouldn't escape me a second time.' The threat was there, and she shivered involuntarily.

'Andrea phoned this morning.'

Ryan leaned against the back of his chair in a deliberately indolent pose that reminded her of a jungle beast poised for attack. One false move, and she'd be in the midst of a battle! 'So Jenkins told me.'

'I was just able to catch a flight by the skin of my teeth.'

A knock at the door ensured a timely interruption, and Natalie watched as Ryan crossed the carpet.

'Tell reception Mrs Marshall will be checking out in fifteen minutes,' he instructed the waiter after taking the tray. 'We should be through here by then.'

'What do you mean—checking out?' she demanded the instant the door closed behind the uniformed figure.

'I have an apartment in Double Bay,' Ryan declared smoothly, seating himself at the table before sparing her a compelling glance. 'We'll stay there.'

'I'm not moving anywhere,' she insisted stormily. 'Michelle is tired and so am I. We're staying here. *You* stay at your apartment.'

His appraisal was swift and impenetrable. 'You'll come with me, even if I have to carry you.'

'Do you know what you are?' she cried, sorely tried, and became positively incensed as a lazy smile creased his rough-hewn features.

'My imagination boggles,' he accorded dryly, and she burst into restrained expostulatory speech.

'A diabolical, feudal—tyrant! You give orders and expect instant blind obedience, and if anyone should dare to so much as question them, you employ force without a thought to the consequences!' Her voice lowered to a vengeful whisper. 'Well—*damn* you, Ryan Marshall! If you want me out of this hotel, you *can* darned well carry me!'

'You think I won't?' he queried silkily, and she gave a bitter laugh.

'You're going to look pretty silly if you do!'

His eyes held a tigerish gleam. 'Oh, I think I'll evoke some misguided sympathy—a child held against one shoulder, and a wife hauled over the other. They'll imagine you as something of a shrew in need of a sound slap or two—and envy me the experience,' he concluded in a hateful drawl.

Anger made her splutter incredulously, 'You wouldn't dare!'

'Try me.'

The temptation to pick up something and hurl it at him was almost too much to resist, and it was only Michelle's presence that put a cautionary brake on her temper. She stood with impotent rage as Ryan calmly ate his meal, then polished it off with the glass of wine which the waiter had thoughtfully supplied.

'Are you ready?'

Natalie threw him a venomous glare. 'No!'

'Pity,' Ryan drawled, his expression lightly mocking. 'I no longer feel in the mood to fight. But since you insist,' he finished with a slight shrug, standing to his feet.

She took an involuntary step backwards as he crossed to the telephone, and she watched in mesmerised fascination as he dialled the required digits before instructing quietly, 'Will you send a porter to Room——' he checked the number from the key-tab and repeated it. 'And call a taxi.' He replaced the receiver and turned towards Natalie. 'Which is it to be?'

There was no choice if she was to retain a

vestige of dignity, and with an angry toss of her head she crossed to the divan and collected her shoulderbag, then stood in angry silence as he scooped Michelle into his arms and preceded her from the room.

In the taxi she maintained an icy silence, and when it despatched them outside a prestigious apartment block she merely took Michelle and followed as he carried their bags.

The elevator rose with swift electronic precision to the uppermost floor, and with a sense of fatalism Natalie moved past him to wait beside the only visible door in sight.

Inside, it reflected an interior decorator's skilful flair, blending essential masculine colours to achieve an understated elegance. Beige thick-tufted carpet and cream textured walls provided an excellent background for the chocolate-brown velour-covered sofas with camel velvet scatter cushions. Splashes of contrast were interspersed on the walls in the form of bold framed prints.

Natalie strolled towards a deep-cushioned sofa and deposited Michelle, then slid the strap of her bag off her shoulder. 'This is what is commonly referred to as the ultimate in bachelor pads,' she observed with thinly-veiled sarcasm. 'I'm almost afraid to ask, but perhaps you'll indulge me— where is the bedroom?'

Ryan slipped a set of keys into his trouser pocket and crossed to an elegantly assembled bar. 'There are two at the end of the hall,' he informed her dryly, reaching for a glass and pouring himself a drink. 'Will you have one?'

'I'll bath Michelle first and settle her down.' She picked up the smaller of the two bags and glanced back at her daughter.

'Go ahead, I'll bring her.'

'Daddy,' Michelle insisted sleepily, fighting to keep her eyes open, and with a husky laugh Ryan left the bar and crossed to the sofa.

'Come on, sleepyhead, he bade, lifting the little girl into his arms. 'Bath and bed, hm?'

The task became a joint effort, and there was a strange aching sensation around the region of her heart as Natalie watched those tiny arms wind themselves up round Ryan's neck as he bent to bestow a goodnight kiss. Even as they moved back from the bed, the drooping eyelids flickered shut, and her breathing tempered into an even beat denoting sleep.

In the lounge she chose a solitary cushioned chair and sank into it to view him warily as he crossed to the bar and retrieved his glass.

'A light wine—or something stronger?'

'Stronger,' she declared succinctly, and saw one eyebrow rise with sardonic amusement.

'On an empty stomach, is that wise?'

Natalie lifted a hand and let her fingers thread through the length of her hair. 'I'm not in the mood for wisdom.' She watched as he poured a measure of spirits into a glass and added a generous splash of soda water before handing it to her.

'It would have been easier if you'd left Michelle with Martha.'

'You sound an echo of Andrea,' she said stiltedly, taking a tentative sip, and she grimaced slightly as the spirits hit the back of her throat.

'The hospital has this number,' Ryan assured her, and took a generous swallow, his eyes enigmatic as they noted each fleeting expression on her delicate features. 'They'll call if there's any change.'

'When are you going back?'

'So eager to be rid of me?' he parried, and she gave an expressive sigh.

'I can't even ask a simple question without it being turned against me!'

'I have to be back on the Coast by Wednesday.'

She raised cool grey eyes to meet his impenetrable gaze. 'I'd like to stay longer. Preferably until Dad is out of hospital.'

'No deal, Natalie,' he refused. 'That could run into several weeks, and I've no intention of permitting your absence for anything approaching that length of time.'

'But I'm his daughter,' she argued. 'I have a right——'

'You're also my wife,' Ryan declared inflexibly, and she uttered a hollow laugh.

'Whose husband doesn't hesitate to exert *his* rights whenever and wherever he pleases!'

'The pleasure isn't exactly one-sided,' he reminded her with droll cynicism, and her action was purely instinctive as she tossed the contents of her glass towards his hateful face.

There was a frightening deliberation in the way he set his glass down on a nearby table, and Natalie watched with hypnotic fascination as he moved towards her. Something in his eyes made her want to scream, but no sound came out.

Without a word he reached for her, drawing her upright and hoisting her over one shoulder to carry her wildly struggling to the bedroom. She rained blows against his back, to any part of that powerful frame that she could reach, and all to no avail, as with a backwards kick with one foot he set the door closed behind him.

'Put me down, you—you *fiend*!'

He allowed her to slide down to her feet, and she winced as his fingers bit painfully into the soft flesh of her arms.

'God help me! You'd try the patience of a saint!' he bit out with barely controlled fury, and the next instant she was hauled with appalling ease across one powerful thigh as he gave her a thorough spanking.

It was an annihilating experience, and one she wouldn't care to have repeated. As Ryan stood her upright she actually felt her body shake with a mixture of suppressed indignation and downright resentment as such high-handedness. She had behaved like a recalcitrant child, and he had reacted accordingly.

'I consider that was long overdue,' Ryan growled harshly, totally unrepentant, and her eyes resembled a storm-tossed sea as she glared up at him.

'You—bastard!' she whispered with bitter vengeance, hating him in that moment to such a degree that it was vaguely frightening. Of all the emotions he was capable of arousing, this was the least enviable.

His smile was totally without humour. 'Be thankful I kept a rein on my temper,' he drawled sardonically. 'My initial instinct was to inflict something far worse.'

'Rape?' Natalie arched with careless disregard. 'I wouldn't let you.'

Something flared in those topaz depths, chilling her to the bone. 'You couldn't stop me.'

An unbidden lump rose to her throat, and she swallowed convulsively. 'Ryan——' Her eyes widened until they resembled huge pools in which genuine fear was reflected.

'Shut up,' he directed with brooding savagery, and his hands closed over the delicate bones of her shoulders as he impelled her forward, then his mouth closed over hers with deadly intent, and the soundless scream remained locked in her throat.

The hardness of his lips crushed hers, forcing them apart, in a ravaging invasion that made her want to cry and rage against him.

To stand quiescent beneath such an onslaught was intolerable, and Natalie beat her fists against his ribs, anywhere she could connect, in an effort to get him to desist. With an ease that was galling Ryan captured first one hand, then the other, and held them together behind her back. Held fast against his hard frame, there was little she could offer by way of resistance, and she suffered his bruising force for what seemed an age before the pressure altered subtly and began to assume a persuasive quality.

Unbidden, a slow fire began to course through her veins, bringing awareness to each separate nerve-end until they tingled with life and appeared to reach out, clamouring for his touch.

Slowly, of their own volition, her arms crept up to encircle his neck, and her fingers curled into the hair that grew low at the base of his nape, caressing, holding his head down to hers in a gesture that betrayed all too vividly her need of him.

Beginning a wild evocative path, his mouth left hers and trailed along her jaw to tease a sensitive earlobe, then pressed a light kiss to each closed eyelid before seeking a tell-tale hammering pulse at the base of her throat. As his mouth wandered slowly downwards she gave an audible moan and arched herself against him, revelling in the depth of emotion he was able to arouse.

One by one, her clothes slowly fell to the floor, and his deep husky laugh greeted her efforts to unbutton his shirt.

'I'll help you,' he husked deeply, and at her faint
blush he bent and bestowed a swift hard kiss to
her trembling mouth. Moments later he lifted her
into his arms and carried her to the bed, where he
led her with consummate ease to the very brink of
ecstasy, pacing her pleasure with his own, until she
wept from the sheer joy of it.

Afterwards she lay within the circle of his arms,
too enervated to move, and she gave a slight sigh
as sleep threatened to claim her. Once again Ryan
had proved that on a physical level they were in
perfect accord. Yet how could their relationship
survive by lust alone? Gradually her eyes closed,
the lashes barely flickering as she gave herself up
to somnolent oblivion.

CHAPTER EIGHT

DURING the next few days Natalie spent most of her time with Andrea at the hospital, providing comfort simply by being there.

Ryan astounded her by completely taking over Michelle, even to supplying an evening meal, and never had she been so grateful for his presence.

On Tuesday afternoon there was a slight change for the better and by evening John Maclean had shown steady improvement. Andrea was still cautious, but her expression held hope that was borne out by the hospital's medical team the next morning.

'Andrea, that's wonderful!' Natalie declared as the news was imparted by phone. 'Yes, I'll tell Ryan. I'll meet you at the hospital in an hour.' She put the receiver down and turned towards the table where Ryan was intent in absorbing the financial section of the daily newspaper.

He looked up as she crossed the room, and his expression was curiously intent. 'Dad's going to be okay,' she told him with a relieved smile, and he inclined his head in silent acknowledgment.

'Good. I'll arrange a late morning flight to Coolangatta.'

Her eyes widened fractionally and a slight frown creased her brow. 'Ryan, I have to stay, surely you must see that?'

'Until Sunday—not a day longer.' His eyes met hers steadily. 'Is that understood?'

She grabbed the reprieve with both hands, agreeing without thought. 'Sunday will be fine.'

'I'll take Michelle with me. The hospital won't allow her in to see John,' he said decisively.

Natalie wasn't sure she liked the idea, but she had to concede that it had some merit. 'All right,' she agreed reluctantly. 'I'll pack' she added, looking at him gravely, knowing she would miss him. Part of her wanted to cry out, 'Don't go', but she overcame the desire to voice those damning words. It wouldn't do to let him think she was falling in love with him again. That way could only lead to disaster. Michelle was something else again, for they had never been apart for longer than a day, and never a night. She felt torn in two, a victim of divided loyalties. Yet she knew there was no other course. She was compelled to stay near her father for a few more days at least.

Ryan crossed to the phone and made two calls, one of them long-distance, while Natalie deftly sorted clothes into a suitcase.

'I'll arrange your flight back,' he told her as they rode the elevator to the ground floor. 'Michelle will be fine,' he added gently as he glimpsed the faint shimmer of tears that threatened to overflow, and she nodded.

'I know. Between Martha and Jenkins, she'll be thoroughly spoiled!' The doors slid open, and a waiting taxi could be seen stationary outside the main glassed entrance. 'I'll phone.'

Ryan paused, shooting her a dark inscrutable glance. 'Dammit, Natalie, this is a hell of a time to become weepily sentimental!' His head bent and he placed a bruising, possessive kiss on her trembling mouth, then he swept through the door without a backward glance and all she could see as the taxi moved away was Michelle's tiny hand waving a frantic farewell.

Damn, damn, *damn*! she muttered to herself,

retracing her steps to the elevator, and she jabbed the button with unnecessary force. She should be rejoicing in her new-found freedom, yet already she felt bereft—almost as if she were a limb that had just been severed from its stalwart trunk. In the weeks since Ryan had forced this ill-fated reconciliation she had prayed for its end—or at least a temporary respite. Now she had it, she found she didn't want it. A sigh escaped her lips. How contrary could she be? One advantage in being alone was that she would have time to evaluate her own emotions. Yet she already knew the answer, and the knowledge didn't help matters at all.

In the apartment she went into the bedroom and attended to her make-up, then after running a brush through the length of her hair she caught up her bag and made for the front door. Scorning the use of a taxi, she walked to the end of the street and caught a bus into the city.

As her father began to improve Natalie limited her visits to fit in with visiting hours, and she often left the apartment early after breakfast to spend the morning exploring the city shops. Andrea would sometimes join her, then after lunch they inevitably caught a taxi to the hospital.

The days were easy to fill. It was the evenings and the long dark hours that appeared to drag. Magazines, books, even the television screen failed to provide more than a fleeting interest, and after spending one night tossing sleeplessly alone in the main bedroom, Natalie moved her things to the smaller guest room.

Michelle's voice on the phone each evening was little more than an excited incomprehensible chatter that was succeeded by Ryan's lazy drawl, and each call caused Natalie to feel more restless than ever. It was Saturday evening, the day before she was due to leave, that the last of Ryan's calls came, and she answered the phone in a breathless rush.

'Natalie? What took you so long?'

Who did he think he was, for heaven's sake? 'I was in the shower,' she explained. 'It's been raining down here, and I got wet walking back from the bus stop.'

There was an infinitesimal silence. 'What the hell were you doing in a bus?'

'I like riding in buses,' she responded civilly, and lifted the towel to rub her hair dry. 'Besides, there wasn't a taxi in sight.'

'Next time, wait for one.' His voice crackled forcibly down the line, and she felt her hackles begin to rise.

'Aren't you being a bit ridiculous?'

'It's a failing where you're concerned,' he drawled. 'Just do as I say, hm?'

'I'll catch a bus if I want to,' she returned sharply, and heard him muffle an oath.

'Your flight leaves at seven tomorrow evening. Check with reservations. They're holding your ticket.'

'I've changed my mind.' The words were out before she had time to think about them. 'I'm not coming back tomorrow.'

'The hell you're not!' he bit out explosively.

'I've decided to stay on a few extra days. Shopping,' she explained sweetly.

'Be on that plane, Natalie,' Ryan directed hardily. 'Or answer to the consequences!'

'What else can you do to me?' she queried simply. Suddenly her act of defiance seemed to lose its appeal. 'You have Michelle,' she continued quietly. 'That alone should be sufficient guarantee that I'll return. Andrea wants to do some shopping, and I'd like to be with her. I'll be back on Tuesday.' She replaced the receiver before he had a chance to comment, and she stood in reflective silence.

What on earth was the matter with her? She wanted to be with Ryan more than anything in the world, yet she had just postponed her return by a further forty-eight hours.

With total disregard for any restraint, Natalie dragged Andrea through a multitude of boutiques on a shopping spree that saw her purchasing another suitcase in which to pack the selection of clothes, shoes and various other sundry items she had bought. Credit cards were produced with careless abandon, and she didn't once give a thought to the size of the bills Ryan would receive as a result. Any pangs of guilt were quickly dampened by the knowledge that he could well afford it!

However, a sense of trepidation descended as the powerful jet touched down at Coolangatta on Tuesday evening, and the butterflies in her stomach began an erratic painful tattoo as she crossed the tarmac with her fellow passengers and entered the airport lounge.

Natalie scanned the large room and its occupants, searching for a familiar head, praying inwardly that it might be Jenkins and not Ryan who had come to meet her. Then a tiny hysterical laugh burst forth from her lips. Maybe no one had come, and she would have to utilise the airport bus to Surfer's Paradise, and catch a taxi home!

It was at that precise moment that she glimpsed a well-groomed head atop a pair of powerful shoulders, and even as she began making her way towards him, Ryan turned and she caught the full force of his tigerish gaze.

All she wanted to do was run and be engulfed in his embrace and feel the warmth of his mouth against her own, but as she drew close she could see a hardness evident in those topaz depths that precluded an affectionate reunion.

Somehow she summoned a smile, an artificial concession that was a mere facsimile, and walked at his side when he crossed to retrieve her bags from the luggage bay.

'I had a wonderful time,' Natalie evinced to no one in particular, and incurred a dark slanting glance.

'I expected another suitcase, at least,' Ryan allowed in an indolent mocking drawl.

'I'm not by nature a big spender,' she offered in explanation. 'However, I'll endeavour to do better next time.'

They reached the car, and Natalie slipped into the passenger seat while Ryan slung her bags into the boot, then he slid in beside her and switched the engine into powerful life.

'How is Michelle?'

'Struggling to stay awake when I left.' He eased out of the parking area and joined the steady stream of traffic moving north along the highway.

'I thought you might have brought her with you. I've missed her.'

'Undoubtedly,' he allowed dryly.

She gave him a quick glance. 'Is that meant to convey censure?'

His shrug was slight. 'What makes you think that?'

Natalie smoothed a stray lock of hair back behind her ear, and let her attention centre on the road ahead. 'You were angry I stayed on an extra few days.'

'Not exactly,' he replied in clipped tones. 'I

don't begrudge you time spent with Andrea, or for that matter, a shopping expedition. I was annoyed because you used it as an excuse for a further act of defiance.'

'You'd prefer me to be an amenable, meek little mouse,' she proclaimed bleakly, and incurred a deep husky laugh by way of response.

'God forbid!'

'And yet there was a time when I bowed to your every wish,' she mused pensively, then slanted him a deep probing glance. 'Now, I seem hell-bent on providing provocation at the least invitation.'

'You do, indeed,' Ryan drawled. 'Have you given a thought to the reason *why*, I wonder?'

Natalie grimaced slightly in the semi-darkness. 'You're the one with all the answers. *You* tell me.'

'Oh no, my sweet. That's one discovery you're going to have to make all on your own.'

There was nothing adequate she could think of by way of reply, and she refrained from commenting for the remainder of the drive home. Ryan, too, appeared in a reflective mood, and after reaching Cronin Island he garaged the car, took her bags from the boot, and followed her indoors.

Jenkins took charge of the luggage at that point, and Ryan indicated the lounge with an indolent sweep of his arm.

'Let's have a drink. I could do with one.'

Natalie stifled the refusal that sprang to her lips, and managed a slight smile. 'I'd like to look in on Michelle first.' She moved towards the stairs, and spared him a glance over her shoulder. 'I'll have something long and cool. I won't be long.' She almost ran upstairs in her haste to escape his disturbing presence, hating herself for the way her contrary senses were behaving at the sight and nearness of him. Wanting to appear cool, calm and collected, she was a shivering mass of nerves knowing that an hour or two from now she would be in his bed.

The door to Michelle's room was closed, and Natalie carefully turned the knob so as not to disturb the little girl as she lay sleeping, her small face angelic in repose, a doll and golliwog flanking her slight body as she lay beneath the covering sheet. A shaft of exultant emotion shot through Natalie as she gazed her fill before bending to bestow the softest of fleeting kisses to the tiny brow, then, content, she retraced her steps and closed the door quietly behind her.

Ryan was standing indolently at ease on the far side of the lounge when she entered it a few brief minutes later, and she crossed to his side and took the glass from his outstretched hand.

'If it's too strong, let me know and I'll add more soda,' he murmured, and she couldn't discern much from his engimatic expression as she took a tentative sip.

'Thank you. It's fine.'

He took a long swallow from the contents of his glass, then cast her an oddly speculative glance. 'I have to fly to the States tomorrow for a few days. Business, I'm afraid. Rick Andreas is coming with me.'

'The wheels of big business, one presumes?'

'What else?' Ryan parried with assumed urbanity, although his eyes were keenly alert, and she proffered a sweet smile.

'I like Lisa. I'll give her a call while you're away, and maybe we can get together for coffee.'

He gave a slight indicative nod of approval. 'She'd enjoy that.'

There was a lengthy silence, and one Natalie felt

she had to break. 'How was Michelle while I was away?'

'Fine. No problems.' His slow smile did strange things to her composure. 'She's a beautiful, well-mannered child.'

Her eyes flickered upward. 'Am I supposed to take that as a compliment?'

'Why not?'

'My goodness,' she managed with every semblance of humour, 'a compliment from the great man himself !'

'Don't be sassy,' he cautioned. 'I may just retaliate!'

'Is that a threat or a promise?'

'Whichever way you choose to take it,' he drawled, and Natalie emptied the contents of her glass in one long swallow before replacing it down on to a nearby table.

'If you'll excuse me, I'm going to take a shower, then go to bed. It's been an exhausting week.'

'No doubt you're relieved at the outcome of your father's operation?'

'Of course,' Natalie responded at once, meeting his penetrating gaze. 'I have to thank you.'

'I shall see that you do,' he slanted lazily, and she felt an unwelcome blush tinge her cheeks.

'Naturally,' she added with droll cynicism, 'I fully expect to have to pay my—er—*dues*, shall we say?'

For a split second his eyes flashed brilliant golden fire, then he bade mockingly, 'Go up to bed, Natalie. I'll join you soon.'

A strangled sound left her throat, then without a further word she turned and walked from the room, gained the stairs, then the upper floor, before closing the door to their room and leaned against it.

Slowly her eyes encompassed the large room with its magnificent furnishings before coming to rest on the silken spread covering the bed. A faint grimace pulled the edges of her mouth. Bed—or rather, *Ryan's* bed—was the reason for her downfall. For it was there that she came alive, exulting in the touch of his hand, his lips, eager to please and be pleased—lost and mindless in the tumult of emotion only he could arouse. It was earth-shattering that one man possessed such power—equally devastating to realise that it could be taken away, as it had three years ago. Yet she had survived. Or had she? She had functioned during that time, but only barely. Now she was akin to a ball back in play on the court, totally at the mercy of the players who directed it, yet at odds at being given no choice.

With a drawn-out sigh she crossed the room and went into the bathroom, discarding clothes with unaccustomed slowness as she turned on the shower, then she stepped beneath its warm spray to cleanse her skin and ease the tension that had set up a slow throbbing ache at the base of her nape.

The whole of life was a game, she mused as she lathered soap over every inch of her body. Something that was manipulated by fate—forces over which there was no control.

If she had never accompanied her friends on holiday to Surfer's Paradise more than three years ago, she wouldn't have met Ryan, and by now she would quite possibly be happily married to someone else. Or maybe she would have made a career for herself and have travelled beyond the fringes of this large continent.

A long shiver slid down her spine, and with a shaky hand she reached out and turned off the water, then sought a nearby towel with which to dry herself. The thought of never having known Ryan was enough to throw her into a state of confused introspection, and the knowledge made her angry. How was it possible to love and hate a man both at the same time? It was crazy!

Towelled dry, she completed her toilette, then slipped a silky nightgown over her head, and emerged into the bedroom to slide beneath the covers. A hand reached out and switched off the bedside lamp, then she closed her eyes against the darkness and drifted within minutes into a dreamless sleep, oblivious to the man who slid in beside her some hours later, and when she woke it was daylight, with the sun filtering warmly through the closed curtains, and all that remained as evidence of her bed having been shared was the thrown-back covers and an imprint on the adjoining pillow.

Natalie greeted Ryan's absence with a sense of relief, grateful for the breathing space it provided. If it hadn't been for her palatial surroundings she could almost believe the past few weeks were a figment of her imagination. Her routine assumed its previous pattern, in that she devoted most of her time to Michelle's welfare as she sought to instil a rudimentary learning programme in preparation for when the little girl would attend kindergarten. She made it a sharing, caring experience and delighted in her daughter's response.

More than anything, Natalie wanted Michelle to grow up as normally as possible—something that would prove difficult when evidence of wealth was all around her. It would be too easy to shower gifts and possessions with careless abandon, and in so doing allow her daughter to believe she could demand anything at will. A careful balance must be preserved at all costs, otherwise a spoilt little termagant would be the result.

Jenkins' presence behind the wheel of the powerful Daimler merely added to the reality of Ryan's status, and Natalie dismissed his insistence to act as chauffeur with a negligent wave of her hand.

'I'm quite capable of driving,' she added in an attempt to appease him. 'My Queensland licence is still current, and besides,' she paused, wrinkling her nose with an impish grin, 'you maintain the illusion of grandeur. If I don't adopt a down-to-earth approach, Michelle will mistakenly believe she's a princess at least!'

'I've been instructed to accompany you,' Jenkins persisted in mild rebuke, and Natalie gave a wry grimace.

'Any particular reason why?'

The manservant chose his words carefully. 'Unemployment is high among the youths frequenting the surfing beaches. They need money to support their carefree lifestyle, and many arrive from out-of-State full of dreams and soon have little more than empty pockets. Security among the wealthy residents is a necessity, not an indulgence.'

Natalie put her head slightly to one side, and subjected him to a steady scrutiny. 'Are you trying to suggest that kidnapping, or abduction, is a possibility?'

'My presence is a precaution against any eventuality,' he responded evenly, and she shook her head slowly.

'I think you're being overly dramatic. This isn't Europe, and Ryan isn't that much of a plutocrat—is he?'

'It isn't my position to comment, except to request you allow me to follow his wishes.'

'Orders, don't you mean?'

'Very well—orders.'

She drew a shaky hand through her hair. 'And if I choose to disregard them?'

'I strongly advise against it,' he responded quietly, and she threw up her hands in a gesture of mute despair.

'Jenkins! I don't want to get you into any trouble, but honestly, all I want to do is browse among the shops in town, then perhaps drive to one of the amusement parks—even explore the outskirts, like Nerang.' Her eyes beseeched him to understand. 'I can't keep you hanging around for most of the day at my beck and call. It isn't fair,' she protested. 'You have plenty of other more worthwhile things to do.'

'Looking after your welfare, and that of your daughter, is what I'm paid to do.'

'As well as attending to the grounds, maintaining all three cars, the shopping——' Natalie reeled off in a rush. 'How can you do any of those things if you're out with me for most of the day?'

'There are any number of private contractors on call for maintenance of the grounds. Ryan's orders were most specific. You have first priority.' Jenkins tempered the words with a kindly smile, but she wasn't amused.

'No matter what he says, I won't be treated like a pampered pet,' she muttered in retort, then offered a conciliatory smile. 'It has nothing to do with you personally. I really enjoy your company.'

'Then why not comply?'

'Because it's a matter of principle,' Natalie insisted stubbornly.

'The car will be ready if you'd care to let me know what time you want to leave.'

'Oh!' she expelled her breath in an angry sigh. 'You're just as bad as he is!'

'It's for your own protection, Natalie. Please believe that,' the older man said gently, and she shrugged her shoulders in defeat.

'If you insist. Shall we say—half an hour?'

The morning was pleasant, with Michelle on her best behaviour, so that the time passed with amazing speed as they strolled through the many arcades before venturing on to the beach for a walk along the sandy foreshore.

As a threesome, they were the recipients of more than idle speculation from several passers-by, and Natalie felt a light laugh erupt with gurgling mirth.

'They're not sure what to make of us,' she giggled softly. 'Are you my father? A doting uncle, perhaps? My—er—benefactor? Or my husband, so much more mature than I, and whom I could only possibly have married for money. For shame!' she mocked, unabashed.

'I prefer to think of you as the daughter I never had,' Jenkins said gently, and she stopped in her tracks and turned towards him.

'Why, Jenkins, how very sweet!' On impulse she leant forward a gave his cheek a quick kiss. 'I'm flattered.'

'I must say how pleased I am that you're back with Ryan again. Martha and I were very upset when you left.'

'It was—just one of those things,' she said a trifle sadly.

There was a slight pause, then he said quietly, 'I'm sorry if I offended you.'

'Good grief, how could you do that?'

'By mentioning something that's none of my business.'

She gave a slight shrug. 'It's all water under the bridge, Jenkins. What counts is that we're together.'

'Have you any plans for this afternoon?'

It was a tactful attempt to divert the conversation, and Natalie was grateful.

'Oh, I'm sure I'll manage to think of something,' she grinned, and he gave a warm smile.

'If you've had enough of the beach, may I suggest we walk along the Esplanade?'

She spared him a quick encompassing glance, then burst into laughter. 'You long-suffering man—I bet you've got sand in your shoes! Own up!'

'You're right,' he grimaced ruefully. 'I'm not exactly dressed for this particular caper.'

'Then back to civilisation and asphalt paving,' Natalie grinned, and scooping Michelle into her arms she turned and led the way to a short flight of steps on her left.

They were about to turn into Orchid Avenue when a bright voice hailed them, and Natalie turned at once to see an attractively dressed young woman crossing the road towards them.

'Lisa, how nice to see you,' she greeted warmly, and received an answering smile in response.

'Likewise. And this must be Michelle.' She gave the little girl a teasing grin. 'Have you been in town long?'

'About an hour and a half,' Jenkins told her, and Lisa tilted her head to one side.

'Would you consider joining me for lunch?'

'I'd love to, but this young lady has a sleep directly after her midday meal,' Natalie proffered with regret, and Jenkins intervened mildly,

'If I might make a suggestion? Allow me to take Michelle home. Martha can feed her and put her to bed, and you can ring me when you want to be brought home.'

'How about it?' asked Lisa, her eyes twinkling with enthusiasm, and Natalie accepted without demur.

'We'll walk to the car,' she declared, her spirits lifting at the thought of a few hours spent in Lisa's company. It would be nice to talk to someone her own age, browse among the boutiques without being conscious of Michelle's distracting presence.

The little girl didn't blink an eyelid on being strapped into her car-seat, and smiled as she waved goodbye when the large car drew away from its parking space.

'Martha and Jenkins have become surrogate parents,' Natalie told him. 'Or perhaps I should amend that to a combination of grandparents and babysitters-in-chief.'

'Do you mind?'

'Not really,' she said. 'It takes a little getting used to. I've had her all to myself for almost two and a half years.'

'Is there anywhere you'd like to go in particular for lunch?' Lisa questioned, and Natalie grinned.

'There are so many new restaurants I'm unaware of, so you lead, and I'll simply follow.'

'You might regret that statement. I have a penchant for seafood, so be warned,' Lisa declared lightly.

'Seafood is fine.'

They ordered a light Moselle, and sipped it tentatively while perusing the menu, then ordered after a leisurely deliberation.

'I've been meaning to call you,' Lisa began. 'I guess you know Rick has gone with Ryan to the States?'

'He did mention it, yes.'

'I was going with them, but flying is out at the moment.' Her eyes positively sparkled. 'It's considered unwise at this crucial stage of pregnancy.'

Natalie's response was genuinely warm. 'I imagine Rick is very pleased.'

'Faintly bemused,' Lisa amended. 'With a history of twins on both sides of the family, I've been warned there's a likelihood I'll follow suit. It's a little too soon to tell, but I'm mentally prepared to buy two of everything!'

The waiter served them each with a starter of prawn salad, refilled their glasses, and discreetly retreated.

'Mmm,' Lisa accorded with evident enjoyment. 'I'll have to watch what I eat, otherwise I'll be adding a few extra unwanted kilos!'

'You're as slim as a reed,' Natalie declared, and the other girl laughed.

'Only because I endeavour to stay that way. Too much indulgence, and I'll have to buy a new wardrobe.'

'I'm sure Rick wouldn't mind,' Natalie opined idly, and gave her attention to the delectable food placed before her. Crumbed scallops and salad greens excellently prepared were a delight to the palate, and followed by a compôte of fresh fruit topped with a dollop of cream served to complete an extremely enjoyable meal.

'Coffee?'

'I don't think I could find room for it, now,' Natalie sighed. 'Perhaps we could have one later?'

'Good idea. Now, I'll take care of the bill,' Lisa determined, and as Natalie made to demur, she smilingly shook her head. 'I insist. Next time I'll allow you to do the honours.'

'In that case, I'll give in gracefully.'

Once outside, they walked to the nearest arcade and idly browsed among the several boutiques before heading for a nearby coffee lounge sporting umbrellaed tables set up outdoors.

'Ah, this is nice.' Lisa sank into a chair and smiled at Natalie. 'We must do this fairly often.'

'I'd love to. Really,' Natalie assured her, and the other girl broke into an engaging grin.

'Rick and Ryan have been friends, as well as business associates, for a long time. It's an added bonus that their respective wives get on well together.' Lisa wrinkled her nose and gave a slight grimace. 'A lot of the women I meet socially are superficial and too wrapped up in themselves to be interested in anyone or anything else.'

'I couldn't agree more,' Natalie said with feeling. 'I can't help thinking I'm on display.'

Lisa laughed. 'You, too?' She gave a slight shrug. 'The first few months after I married Rick are something I wouldn't want to repeat.'

Natalie sipped the last of her coffee and replaced her cup down on to its saucer, enjoying the slight breeze that had sprung up.

'I'm afraid I'm going to have to leave within the next few minutes,' Lisa excused herself regretfully as she spared a glance at her watch. 'I've an appointment with my gynaecologist. His rooms are not far from here.' She drained her coffee and stood to her feet. 'The men are due back the day after tomorrow. I'll get Rick to arrange something with Ryan, and we'll get together for dinner. I'll ring and let you know.'

Natalie caught hold of her shoulderbag and paid the hovering waitress, then walked with Lisa to the main highway where they parted to go in opposite directions.

It was such a nice day—too nice to bother

Jenkins again with the car. In any case, she felt like walking, and it wasn't far. The exercise would do her good!

She set off at a leisurely pace and reached the Chevron bridge, glimpsing the sparkling waters of the river flowing below as she crossed to the other side. Small craft sped noisily towards the river's mouth, and there was a cruise boat in the distance en route to the many waterways that were a tourist feature of the Coast.

The main shopping centre on Chevron Island was busy with traffic, and she took care before crossing at a main intersection, then turned into the street leading to Cronin Island.

She hadn't walked one block when a slight noise alerted her attention, and turning, she caught sight of a car travelling at considerable speed very close to the kerb. It was a large nondescript sedan with tinted windows, and a split second later she gave a cry of alarm as it appeared to head straight for her, neither slowing nor attempting to stop.

It had to be out of control, and in a moment of blind horror she sidestepped out of its oncoming path, feeling a rush of air whoosh past as she fell to the ground.

Then it was gone, and she lay still, unaware of any pain, but feeling slightly dazed and very shaken. Slowly she rose to her feet and reached down to retrieve her shoulderbag, then she cast a glance up the street to see if there were any witnesses, but there were none. Not a solitary soul in sight! she thought hysterically.

Gingerly she stepped forward. The small bridge leading to Cronin Island was just up ahead beyond the slight curve in the road, and once she reached that she was barely one hundred metres from home.

Five minutes later she pressed the intercom button beside the locked gates, and leaned against the solid concrete wall as she waited for Jenkins or Martha to answer.

'Marshall residence. Would you please state your name?'

'It's Natalie, Martha,' she said shakily. 'Can you let me in?'

'Good heavens——'

Those were the last words she heard as a black inky void descended, and she slid to the ground in a crumpled heap.

CHAPTER NINE

WHEN Natalie came to she was lying in bed, and there was a strange man holding her hand.

'Who are you?' Did she speak those words? They sounded strange, almost as if they belonged to someone else, and as for her head—it felt light and woolly, not her own at all!

'Dr Henson, Mrs Marshall,' he told her quietly. 'How do you feel?'

'I'm not sure,' she owned shakily, and he gave a slight smile of reassurance.

'I'll conduct a thorough examination now that you're awake. Are you in any pain?'

Was she? She moved cautiously, but nothing hurt. 'No.'

'Can you remember what happened?'

Natalie gave a brief nod, then revealed what had transpired. Martha stood in the background, her kind features creased with anxiety, and Natalie spared her a smile. 'I'm all right—honestly. Just a bit shaken.'

'We'll see, shall we?' The doctor began his examination, and when it was completed he stood to his feet and closed his bag. 'You've been very lucky, in my opinion. A few grazes, some bruising, and shock. Bedrest for the next eighteen hours,' he instructed, then gave a slight smile. 'You'll have a few aches and pains tomorrow, but I'll check on those when I call in the morning.'

Natalie's lids flickered wide. 'Is that necessary?'

'I'm sure Mr Marshall will think so,' he declared, then he turned towards Martha. 'There's no concussion, but if you're concerned at all, you have my number.'

Jenkins could be seen hovering in the hall as Martha opened the door, and Natalie shook her head in disbelief. 'Such a fuss! I'm perfectly fine. You heard the doctor.'

'Would you like something to drink? A nice hot cup of tea with plenty of sugar will do you good,' the older woman suggested as she crossed to the bed.

'Is Michelle still asleep?' On receiving an affirmative nod, Natalie gave a sigh of relief. 'Thank heavens for that! I suppose Jenkins carried me inside?'

'That he did,' Martha declared. 'You gave us both the shock of our lives!'

'It was such a nice day, I thought I'd walk,' Natalie explained. 'I didn't anticipate being the inadvertent victim of some lunatic driver.'

'Ryan won't be pleased.'

'Does he have to know?'

Martha slowly shook her head. 'Jenkins is going to put a call through as soon as the doctor leaves. I'll go and make that tea. I could do with a cup myself!'

With a bit of luck, Ryan would be unreachable and therefore remain in ignorance until his return home. Natalie did a swift mental calculation, and came up with Saturday—which was *tomorrow*.

Despite all opposition, Martha insisted on serving Natalie dinner on a tray in bed, and afterwards Michelle was allowed to visit her for a while. The little girl's eyes were huge as she stood solemnly beside the bed, and it took some persuasion before she could be led to her own room across the hall.

Natalie idly leafed through some magazines

Martha provided, but she couldn't settle to do more than scan a few of the articles before discarding one glossy scribe after another. Even the portable television Jenkins had set up on a stand at the end of the bed didn't hold her interest for long, and shortly after eight she slipped out of bed and went into the bathroom with the intention of having a shower. A few aches were beginning to make themselves felt as the bruising started to come out, and the hot water would surely ease them a little.

Her eyes fell on the oval bathtub with its gold-plated taps, the bottles of essence, and she changed her mind. A quick turn of her wrist and water gushed out of the taps, filling the room with steam, and she added essence before slipping out of her nightgown, then she stepped into the hot fragrant water.

She soaked until the water cooled and she was on the verge of adding more hot water when there was a soft knock at the door.

'Ryan is on the phone,' Martha called, and Natalie gave a prodigious sigh.

'Tell him I'm in the bath.' She knew it wouldn't make the slightest difference, but maybe she could put off the inevitable.

'He insists on speaking to you,' the older woman declared.

'Couldn't I be asleep? I don't feel up to answering a whole lot of questions.'

'Jenkins has already given him all the details. Being so far away, it's only natural he wants to hear from you personally.'

Natalie stood up and reached for a towel, and after drying most of the excess moisture from her body she wrapped the towel sarong-wise round her slim curves and opened the door.

Martha's face showed concern, and a certain amount of compassion. 'Get back into bed. There's an extension there.' Her smile was kindly. 'I'll bring up some warm milk and brandy. It will help you sleep.'

Natalie crossed to the bed and sat down, then with a sense of trepidation she reached for the receiver. 'Ryan? How are you?'

'More to the point—how are *you*?' His voice held restrained anger, and she resorted to flippancy by way of defense.

'I'm still in one piece, if that's what you want to know. No damage to report, just a few scratches and some bruising. In other words, I'm fine.'

'Bill Henson assures me you were fortunate to have come off so lightly,' he drawled, and she demanded incredulously—

'Did you ring him?'

'Of course. Did you expect me not to?'

'Why? Jenkins gave a full report.'

'Assuredly,' Ryan said abruptly. 'He rang me immediately.'

Natalie changed the receiver to her other hand and pushed back her hair from where it had fallen to cover part of her face. 'It had nothing to do with Jenkins,' she began quietly. 'I hope you haven't implied that he was in any way to blame.'

'Dammit, Natalie,' he groaned softly, 'why *walk* home, for God's sake?'

His tone made her stomach muscles contract with tension, and a slow-burning anger came to the surface in retaliation. 'Can't you leave the post-mortem until tomorrow? Your concern is gratifying, but quite honestly, you're giving me a headache!'

His muffled oath was barely audible, and she didn't wait for him to comment further. 'I'm rather tired. Goodnight.' With that she replaced the receiver, then sat staring at the phone half expecting it to ring, and when after several minutes it didn't, she rose and extracted a nightgown, then returned and slid into bed.

'I've brought you some Paracetamol tablets to ease the pain,' Martha told her as she entered the room. 'Make sure you drink the milk. If you take my advice, you'll try to get some sleep.'

Natalie pulled a face, but obediently took the glass from the proffered tray. 'I feel like a child,' she grumbled, tempering the words with a slight smile.

'I'm going to sleep in the next room. Then if you need anything, or Michelle wakes during the night, I'll be close by.'

The older woman's kindness overwhelmed her, and her eyes filled with tears. 'Thank you.' She took the glass and sipped its contents, swallowed the tablets, then when the glass was empty she placed it on to the tray and slid down into a comfortable position. 'I feel drowsy already,' she murmured. 'Goodnight. And—thank you,' she added gently. 'You're very kind.'

When Natalie woke in the morning she felt stiff and sore. The slightest movement made her wince with pain, and she ran a tub full of hot water in which to soak.

Martha brought her breakfast shortly after eight, and Michelle put in an appearance the minute she was permitted. Dr Henson called at nine, examined her and pronounced her fit enough to get up after lunch.

The day passed slowly, although as evening drew near Natalie was aware of a build-up of nervous tension. Ryan's arrival was imminent, and she dreaded the initial confrontation. Jenkins left with the car at eight, and within minutes she elected to retire upstairs on the pretext of going to bed.

It was sheer cowardice, she knew, but the thought of facing him was more than she could bear. With a bit of luck, she would be asleep when he returned.

Instead, she tossed and turned, unable to get comfortable, and instead of relaxing, she grew more tense with every passing minute.

The lights of the car as it swung into the driveway threw a momentary beam that reflected through the drapes at the window, filling the room with a subdued glow, then it was gone, and she turned on her side, facing away from the door in the hope that when he did enter the room he would assume she was asleep.

It didn't work that way, and she cursed herself for being such a fool in thinking that it might.

Minutes later the door opened and she sensed rather than heard him come in. A switch clicked as the bedside lamp sprang to light, then the side of the bed depressed with his weight.

'Natalie?'

Pretence was an ineffectual weapon, and she didn't attempt to use it. 'I was trying to get to sleep.'

'I'm sure you were,' Ryan drawled enigmatically, and she responded waspishly,

'Then why disturb me?'

'Your claws are showing, kitten,' he mocked sardonically, and leaning towards her he placed a hand either side of her shoulders. 'I do believe you're all right, after all.'

'Do you want to inspect the evidence? Count every scratch and bruise?' she demanded tritely, and heard his soft chuckle.

'What an interesting idea. Would you comply, I wonder?'

'Like hell!' she responded inelegantly, and swallowed the sudden lump that rose to her throat as his fingers trailed down her cheek.

'My sweet little idiot,' he murmured gently. 'I'm almost afraid to leave you alone. Do you know how fortunate you were not to be seriously hurt?'

'I'm sorry if I caused you concern,' she said stiffly, and Ryan gave an audible groan, then bent low to place his mouth against the side of her neck.

'Next time I go away, I'm taking you with me. At least then I can keep an eye on you.'

'I'm not a child to be watched and guarded every waking moment,' she retorted, then was unable to say anything further as his mouth moved to close over her own in a kiss that was gently possessive.

Minutes later he gathered her on to his lap, and she was unable to prevent a faint gasp of pain as his hands closed over her ribs.

She saw his eyes narrow, then her own widened into huge grey pools as he carefully slid aside the straps of her nightgown.

'Sweet mother in heaven!' Ryan breathed emotively as he caught sight of the dark bruises over most of her ribcage. 'Are there any more like that?'

'I haven't really looked,' Natalie professed, then she gave a startled gasp as he leant down and gently kissed each and every mark. It was a tantalisingly evocative experience, and one that stirred her senses, bringing them alive until they pulsated with latent warmth.

'In a few days' time, we're going away,' Ryan told her quietly. 'Just the two of us. Rick owns a small island off the Great Barrier Reef. It's remote, yet possesses an excellent deep anchorage harbour. Jenkins will stock up the cruiser, and we'll spend a few lazy days on board. Does that hold any appeal?'

The thought of spending every hour in each twenty-four with him sounded warning bells of a kind Natalie daren't ignore. He was capable of weaving his own potent brand of magic—something she could deal with in small doses. But several days was something else, let alone the *nights*!

'Indulge me, Natalie,' he smiled gently. 'I'm in need of a holiday.'

She swallowed compulsively, knowing that fate played a large part in her destiny. What lay between them had to be resolved one way or another. 'In that case,' she said shakily, 'who am I to refuse?'

The cruiser edged its way along the Nerang River, then negotiated the tricky channels by the Spit before heading north.

It was a beautiful day, hot, yet a light breeze did much to ease the sting of the sun's rays.

Natalie had elected to wear a bikini, with a wrap-around skirt which could be removed if it got too hot later on. Ryan looked totally at ease at the controls, his powerful torso bare except for a pair of cotton shorts. Despite working indoors he had managed to acquire a deep tan, and the sight of him almost took her breath away.

She felt relaxed and at ease, almost as if these few days held something special. It was strange, but she knew that whatever had happened before had become a thing of the past. There was only *now*, and the prospect of their future together.

It took five hours to reach the small island—one among so many others, that Natalie wondered how Ryan could possibly claim it to be their intended destination.

'Shall we eat?' she asked as he secured the controls and released the anchor.

'Hungry, are you?' Ryan smiled, and she wrinkled her nose at him.

'Aren't you?'

'Hmm—but not for food.' His glance roved over her slim curves with apparent appreciation, and she blushed at his intended meaning.

'I'm not sure this holiday is a good idea. All this fresh air and sunshine, with too much time on our hands and nothing to do.'

Ryan's eyes were filled with laughter as he gazed at her. 'I can think of plenty!'

She reached for her discarded towel and bunched it into a ball and threw it at him. 'Wretch! I'm going down into the galley to prepare some lunch. You can watch the seagulls.'

'I'd much rather watch *you*.'

Shaking her head slowly, she turned and made for the short flight of steps leading down into the well-appointed cabin. She took iced cans from the refrigerator, lemonade for herself and beer for Ryan, then set about making a salad to go with the cold meat Martha had provided. Crunchy bread rolls completed the meal, and she set the small table with a cloth before adding cutlery, then called that it was ready.

'Mmm, that looks good,' Ryan murmured as he slid his lengthy frame into the cushioned seat, and she gave a slight shrug.

'It isn't Cordon Bleu fare, but it should taste all right.'

'As good as you?'

'Really, you have a one-track mind!' She slid in opposite him and picked up her knife and fork.

'The wounds of the past go deep. Too deep, Natalie?'

The softness of his voice was deceptive, but there was no advantage in pretending. 'A week ago I would have said yes,' she began slowly.

'And now?'

'I don't know.' She looked at him, meeting his steady gaze, and offered quietly, 'A lot has happened since I came back. I need time to think.'

'We also need to talk.'

There was a measurable silence, and one Ryan broke by stating irrefutably, 'First, let's get rid of the largest bogey of all—Simone.' His gaze was startlingly direct.

Natalie took a sip of lemonade in an attempt to give herself the breathing space necessary. 'Perhaps it's best left alone,' she voiced a trifle shakily.

'I don't agree.'

'Couldn't we leave it until tomorrow?' Or the day after, or maybe not at all, she begged silently, not sure she wanted to pursue the subject. It brought back too many painful memories.

'That particular young woman almost destroyed our marriage,' he voiced hardily.

'That was a long time ago,' she said steadfastly. 'I was very young—not only in years, but in experience.'

'I was confident I could shield you from anything and everything,' Ryan said quietly, and she drew a deep calming breath.

'Simone can be very convincing.'

'You ran away. Have you any conception what I went through trying to find you?'

There was one question she had to ask, and courage gave her the necessary impetus. 'Did you never once consider divorce?'

His eyes didn't waver. 'No.'

'I—see,' she said slowly, and he gave a wry smile.

'Do you, Natalie?'

Her eyes became faintly pensive, and she flicked back a stray lock of hair in a purely defensive gesture. 'I feel as if I'm caught up in a whirlpool!'

His eyes gleamed with devilish humour, and a husky laugh sounded deep in his throat. 'You'll come out of it soon. I give you my word.'

The weather proved idyllic, and although a few clouds banked up in the sky, the sun triumphed, bestowing in its benevolence a warm basking glow.

Natalie fished with Ryan, teasing him mercilessly when her catch outweighed his, and they swam, sunbathed, ate, made love, then when the sun went down they made love again, delighting in the pleasure each was able to give the other.

On the third day they lifted anchor and made for the northern point of Stradbroke Island, where they spent a further two days, then regretfully set a course for home.

CHAPTER TEN

MICHELLE was overjoyed to see them, and Ryan listened to her childish, and for the most part indistinguishable chatter with apparent solemnity, sparing Natalie a quick musing gleam across the table as he endeavoured to give his daughter and his breakfast equal attention.

Natalie was unable to prevent the faint tingling blush that stole over her cheeks as she met his smiling gaze, and her eyes were wise and luminous when he rose to his feet minutes later and bestowed a brief hard kiss prior to leaving the house.

Michelle scrambled on to her knee and reached for a finger of toast left on Natalie's plate, consuming it with relish. 'Daddy gone to work,' she chanted in a sweet sing-song voice, and Natalie hugged the small body close.

'Yes, darling. He'll be back in time for tea.'

Solemn wide eyes regarded her unblinkingly. 'We stay home?'

'Well,' Natalie deliberated with a wide smile, 'we could go out, if you like. Suppose we get Jenkins to take us to the shopping centre close to Broadbeach?'

'Cake and fishes,' Michelle declared promptly, and Natalie laughed, hugging her close.

'Very well, imp. We'll have lunch out on the verandah of the coffee shop so that you can watch the fishes in the pond. Then home for a nap, okay?'

' 'kay,' the tot agreed engagingly.

They left shortly after ten-thirty in the Daimler with Jenkins at the wheel and were deposited outside one of the large department stores in the Pacific Fair shopping complex.

'Twelve-thirty will be fine,' Natalie advised as the older man retrieved Michelle's stroller from the boot and set it upright on the pavement.

'I'll be here before that, just in case the little one gets overtired.' He smiled and returned Michelle's wave before slipping in behind the wheel, and Natalie slung the strap of her bag over her shoulder and eased her way with the stroller towards the complex centre.

It was a beautiful day. The sun was hot, but not unpleasantly so. Shoppers wandered the bricked lanes without any sense of haste, and Natalie kept their pace, pausing now and then to browse at an attractive window display before moving on.

'Drink,' Michelle began, adding a plaintive, 'please!'

They were close to a replica of a Cotswold cottage which specialised in Devonshire cream teas and had several tables and chairs set up outdoors beneath a large canopy, and Natalie crossed the small bridge beneath which water flowed from a picturesque waterwheel towards the main pond. She chose a table close to the fenced area and set Michelle on a chair where she could see the goldfish, then ordered a can of lemonade and an iced coffee.

They had visited this complex on two previous occasions, and now she listened attentively as Michelle pointed with excitement to one particularly large red fish they had affectionately named 'Granddaddy'. The fact that there were several fish equally large was something Natalie didn't reveal. There was time enough for the loss of childish fantasy.

The drink consumed, they completed a circle of the shops before heading for the terraced verandah overlooking the pond for lunch. The coffee lounge was well patronised, and after selecting sandwiches Natalie secured an empty table.

The past hour and a half had passed swiftly. In a further five hours Ryan would be home, and she was unable to still the faint smile that softened her lips at the thought his presence evoked. The few days they had spent on Rick's island had been idyllic, something she would treasure for the rest of her life. There was a tremendous feeling of well-being in having come full circle from love, through all the misunderstandings, the bitterness, to the wealth of happiness they now shared. Perhaps it was a lesson one had to learn in the school of life, she perceived, that love is a gift to be treated with the utmost care to ensure it continued to flourish. Something beyond the physical and spiritual emotions, becoming an inextricable entity interwoven with trust and fidelity.

'More fish, Mummy!'

Natalie came out of her reverie, and smiled down at the little girl happily finishing the last of her sandwich. 'Yes, darling.' She drained her coffee, then steadied Michelle's glass so that it didn't spill. 'When you've had your drink we'd better go.' She spared a glance at her watch and saw that it was almost twelve-thirty. 'Jenkins will be waiting for us.'

He was, but with the utmost patience, and Michelle obediently scrambled into her car-seat, her face wreathed in smiles as Natalie fastened the straps.

The stroller placed in the boot, Jenkins slipped

behind the wheel, and almost immediately the little girl regaled him with the morning's events in a ceaseless childish spiel which lasted until the moment he brought the large vehicle to a halt in the driveway.

'Right, my girl,' Natalie grinned as she released the tot and scooped her into her arms. 'Face, hands, teeth, then into bed with you!' She walked to the door, then crossed the foyer towards the stairs. 'When you wake, we'll swim in the pool and I'll give you another lesson. Just think how surprised Daddy will be when he finds out you can swim.'

'Like the fishes,' Michelle giggled, and Natalie laughed and buried her face against the little girl's neck.

'You wriggle like a fish,' she declared as she set the child down to her feet in the bathroom. Within minutes she had her clean, then divested of outer clothing, she carried her through to the bedroom and slipped the small body between cool sheets before crossing to draw the drapes at the window. 'Sleep tight, angel.'

' 'bye, Mummy.'

Natalie retraced her steps to the lower ground floor where she collected a pad and pen with which to write a letter to her father and Andrea. Sliding open the screened door, she crossed the courtyard and sat down at one of the outdoor tables.

It was pleasantly warm beneath the shady canvas umbrella, and she flipped open the pad and began to record a newsy account of the past week, adding in detail various anecdotes related to Michelle.

'Excuse me, Natalie but there's someone to see you.'

She glanced up with faint surprise at the sound of Martha's voice, and caught the older woman's slight perplexion.

'It's Miss Vesey.'

Natalie gave a slight grimace, uttering a barely audible 'Damn!' as she laid down her pen. 'I suppose I can't be out?' she hazarded ruefully, not relishing the prospect of seeing Simone, let alone attempting to entertain her.

' 'fraid not, sweetie,' a brightly pitched voice drawled from the wide screen door, and into the sunshine walked its elegantly-clad owner. 'I decided not to wait,' she explained with considerable hauteur to Martha, then encountered Natalie with a wide brittle smile. 'After all, I know this house like the back of my hand.'

Martha's expression was civil, but only just, and her displeasure was evident by the faint tightening of her lips the instant before she turned back towards Natalie.

'Would you like me to bring something cool to drink?'

'Do that,' Simone instructed with a careless fluttering hand as she crossed to sit at the table opposite Natalie. 'You know what I usually have.'

The older woman was politely stoical. 'You'll have to refresh my memory, Miss Vesey. It's some time since you last visited this house.'

A soft tinkling laugh was at variance with the annoyance expressed in those brilliant dark eyes. 'Really, Martha,' she chided with a slight moue, 'there's no need to be discreet! Natalie knows all about Ryan's fascination for me.' She arched a sparkling glance towards her victim, and taunted, 'Don't you, darling?'

Dear Lord, what was this viperous witch up to? Natalie took in the over-bright eyes, the slender scarlet-tipped nails engaged in extracting a cigarette from its elegant gold case, and drew a deep steadying breath. If Simone had possessed the foreknowledge to time her attack for the previous week, it might have had the desired effect, but she was that many days too late.

'I'll have iced soda water, Martha,' Natalie said quietly. She needed a clear head to deal with the enemy—for Simone was surely that!

'Make mine vodka on ice with a splash of bitters and lime.'

Martha's obvious reluctance to leave them alone was oddly touching, and Natalie swung slowly back to meet Simone's brittle gaze.

'Is this a social visit?' Her voice was incredibly polite, and distant.

'My dear—no,' the other woman denied, and exhaling a stream of smoke into the air she leaned forward so that her elbows rested on the table. 'Surely you've guessed why I'm here?' A malevolent gleam lanced the distance between them. 'You're not exactly dumb.'

Natalie unconsciously eased back against her chair until she felt its support and endeavoured to appear relaxed. 'May I take that as a compliment?'

'You don't learn, do you?' Simone demanded acidly.

'On the contrary,' Natalie answered with considerable poise, 'I've learned a great deal.'

'Oh, I'll concede you're three years older,' her aggressor agreed with a derogatory laugh. 'But you're still incredibly naïve.'

'I think you'll find I'm somewhat more mature than you give me credit for,' Natalie managed evenly, treading the verbal distance with care.

Simone tilted her head slightly and fixed Natalie

with an unwavering stare that was unnerving to say the least. 'Really?'

The tension was broken by Martha's return, and Natalie gave the older woman a grateful smile as the tray of drinks was placed on the table.

'Would you care for something to eat? I've just taken a batch of scones from the oven.'

'Nothing,' Simone refused with chilling dismissal, and a perverse streak caused Natalie to voice with warm enthusiasm,

'I'd love one, split, with jam and cream, if it isn't too much trouble.'

'Of course not.

'Really, Natalie!' Simone chided with thinly-veiled sarcasm. 'Martha is merely a servant. Treat her like a friend, and you'll find she'll take over.'

Natalie picked up the frosted glass and took a long cool sip before replacing it back on to the table. 'Jenkins and Martha have been with Ryan for a long time,' she said steadily. 'As for running the house, Martha does that with the utmost efficiency, and completely to my satisfaction.'

Simone sipped at her vodka, and eyed Natalie with an odd speculative gleam over its rim. 'My, my! Perhaps you have grown up a little. Your claws are showing!'

You ain't seen nothing yet! Natalie jeered silently. A tiny smile lifted the edges of her mouth, and her eyes were clear and without guile. 'You'll find they're quite sharp.'

'Is that a warning of some sort?'

Natalie lifted her glass and took another appreciative sip before responding. 'If you care to think so.'

Anger tightened the other woman's face into an unattractive mask. 'I don't take threats lightly.'

Natalie's head lifted slightly as she met Simone's smouldering gaze. 'Neither do I.'

'How am I threatening you?'

'Aren't you?'

'You silly little bitch!' Simone snapped viciously. 'The only reason you're here is because of a stupid mistake.'

'Apparently I'm guilty of several,' Natalie said a trifle flippantly. 'Perhaps you'd care to elucidate?'

'Michelle,' the other declared succinctly. 'Your daughter, and supposedly Ryan's.' She gave a high-pitched laugh that sounded faintly off-key. 'In these modern times, you certainly goofed, didn't you, sweetie?' Her eyes glittered dangerously. 'Or was it all part of a carefully thought out plan?'

It was perhaps as well that Martha came on the scene at that precise moment, or Natalie's reserve of patience might have flown the coop!

'Will that be all?' the valued servant queried, her face creased with anxiety, and Simone snapped out,

'Oh, for God's sake! Leave us alone, will you?'

The older woman drew herself to her fullest height, and her bosom fairly quivered with rage. 'I take my orders from Mrs Marshall, not the likes of you!'

'Thank you for the scones, Martha,' Natalie said quietly, her eyes remarkably steady. 'Would you mind checking on Michelle for me? She's due to wake soon.'

For a moment Martha appeared doubtful whether she should leave, then ignoring Simone she gave Natalie a troubled smile. 'If she wakes, I'll keep her amused inside the house.'

'Do that,' Simone declared viciously. 'I can't stand little brats.'

Obviously that was too much for Martha, for with considerable aplomb she turned and subjected Simone to a raking stare. 'Praise God, Ryan had the good sense not to marry you.'

'If he had, you certainly wouldn't still be here!'

Martha's mouth tightened into a thin line, then exercising great restraint she made a dignified exit, and the minute she was out of sight Simone burst into furious speech.

'That woman is just too much!'

'I think you've outstayed your welcome,' Natalie observed, standing to her feet. 'I'll see you to the door.'

'I haven't said what I came to say.'

'Forgive me. I consider you've already said too much.'

'Oh, darling, I haven't even started yet!'

Natalie refrained from saying so much as a word, then after a measurable silence she sank back into her chair. 'I'm all ears, Simone. Get whatever it is off your chest, then leave.'

Out came the cigarettes and lighter, and not until one slim tobacco tube was lit to her satisfaction did the words flow.

'It's relatively simple. I want Ryan.'

Natalie's eyes were remarkably level as she viewed the dark-haired sophisticated beauty. 'Does Ryan want you?'

'I wouldn't be here if he didn't.'

'Am I supposed to fit in with your scheme and lamely offer to divorce him?'

'It would help. However, he's wealthy enough to employ someone to manufacture evidence against you.'

'Adultery?'

An elegant stream of smoke slowly wafted between them, and Simone reached for her half-empty glass and proceeded to drain its contents. 'You catch on fast.'

'What if I won't comply?'

'You will. I supplied you with sufficient evidence three years ago. Your return hasn't changed anything.'

'Have you never heard the adage—"once bitten, twice shy"?'

'Are you going to be difficult?' Winged eyebrows arched with sardonic cynicism. 'I wouldn't advise it, sweetie.' A vengeful gleam entered Simone's eyes, making them appear malevolent and infinitely dangerous. 'Next time you're out walking I'll ensure you get more than a fright!'

Comprehension gave way to concern. 'You put my life at risk, deliberately! That's a criminal offence.'

'You'd have to prove it first.'

'You must want Ryan very badly,' Natalie said quietly, and Simone gave a hollow laugh.

'I had him, once. Then you came on the scene.' Her eyes gleamed with a mixture of molten fire and ice. 'A silly teenager from the country. God! You had *nothing* compared to what I could give him.'

'Except, maybe—love?'

'What has that got to do with it?'

'Everything, I imagine,' Natalie said dryly.

'I satisfied him on a physical level.' A look of pure enmity made Simone's features appear ugly. 'Whereas *you*, so lily-white and virginal, could hardly have known what it was all about!'

'Ryan is an excellent tutor,' Natalie remarked, not really wanting to pursue with such invective. Yet this was war, if only a verbal one, and had to be led to its ultimate conclusion.

'I'm sure I could provide more titillating tricks than you ever dreamed were possible!'

'Lust alone is an empty emotion. Only when it's accompanied by love does it become something beautiful.'

'Don't hand me that sentimental rubbish! Look around you,' Simone spat vengefully. 'This house, the cars, apartments—even the cruiser goes into a cool six figures! Who cares about *love*?'

'I do,' Natalie said with quiet conviction, and for a moment she looked incredibly sad. 'Whatever you believe to the contrary, it was Ryan who made the running in our relationship. Even when I expressed doubts, he overruled them.' Courage gave her the strength to go on. 'I was overwhelmed in those first few crucial months after Ryan married me. I'd never met anyone like him, and all these trappings appeared like a giant fairytale. Instead of deriving pleasure from them, they rose between us like an insurmountable barrier. Given a choice, I'd have preferred to have been without them. At least then I could have felt able to compete on an equal level.' A drawn-out sigh left her lips, and she forced a slight smile. 'As it was, I became confronted at every turn with sophisticated socialites who for the most part didn't care a fig about me personally. I knew that, and so did you. What was more, you wanted what I appeared to have—*Ryan*. Or rather, Ryan's possessions. You played your hand well, Simone. Like a gullible fool, I believed every word you said and ran as far and as fast as my legs would carry me.' She paused, and idly traced the pattern on the wrought-iron table with her finger. 'However, this time I'm not running.'

'You'll stay and be humiliated?'

'Why should I be humiliated?' she parried.

'I can take Ryan from you as easily as——'
Simone clicked her fingers in the air with a decisive
snap—'that.'

'If that's true, why didn't he instigate a legal
separation and then divorce me?'

'Because he was embittered with marriage,'
Simone vented furiously. 'However, given time, I
could have won him round.'

'Well, your time just ran out,' Natalie said
carefully, making sure she enunciated her words
with clear distinction as she continued, 'I love
him—very much. There's Michelle, whom neither
of us would give up easily. And there'll be another
child before the years's end, unless I'm mistaken.'

The fury in Simone's face was something
frightening to see, and for a moment Natalie
fought an instinctive desire to back away. Quietly
she stood her ground, her gaze unwavering,
outwardly calm yet defensively on the alert.

Even so, she was unprepared for the hand that
snaked out and dealt a stinging blow to her left
cheek, almost unbalancing her. Blindly she
reached for the edge of the table in an attempt to
steady herself, and felt her vision blur as tears
welled at the pain Simone had managed to inflict.

'You smart, conniving little bitch! I hate you—
hate you, do you hear?' The words streamed out
with low guttural invective, and Natalie lifted a
shaky hand to brush the excess moisture from her
eyes.

'I think you'd better leave.'

Natalie heard Jenkins' voice and slowly turned
to face him, seeing the silent anger expressed in his
usually kind features. Thank God for his
intervention! Simone had gone beyond rage to the
brink of not being responsible for her actions.

'I'll leave when I damn well please!' Dark hair

swung in a slow arc as her head turned towards the manservant. 'Now get out. I haven't finished yet.'

'You are no longer welcome in this house, Miss Vesey,' Jenkins asserted with calm inflexibility, and Natalie saw him move until he stood between her and Simone. 'If you won't leave of your own accord, I shall have to employ force.'

'Lay a finger on me, and I'll have you up for assault!'

'I don't think so,' a deep drawling voice intervened, and Natalie's eyes flew to the tall figure moving towards them.

'Ryan! Oh, thank God you've come!' Simone cried, and a whole flood of words flowed from her lips, interspersed with convulsive sobs. 'It's been awful—she's been so horrible—saying terrible things——'

Natalie stood in stunned silence, part of her brain registering with devilish humour that Simone was stealing *her* lines! Like an invisible spectator she observed the tableau, noting the two men's stance with interest. One defensive; the other dangerous, resembling a jungle tiger about to spring. Simone's acting excelled itself. Indeed, if Natalie hadn't been an unwilling participant and evidenced for herself such bitter invective, she would have believed every word that came out of the other woman's mouth!

Ryan appeared to listen, but his eyes were on Natalie, not Simone. When the torrent of words came to a halt, his voice was almost deadly in its intent as he stressed with chilling abruptness,

'Jenkins will escort you to your car. If you so much as come within speaking distance of my wife again, or attempt to threaten her in any way, I will personally see to it that you never receive an

invitation from any of the Coast's social echelon.'
His eyes were pitiless and totally without mercy. 'If
you possess an ounce of sense, you'll re-locate
yourself elsewhere.'

'But you loved me! I know you did!'

His silence became an almost tangible thing, and
Natalie unconsciously held her breath.

'I used you, in much the same manner you used
me,' he corrected with silky detachment. 'It was
over many years ago—long before Natalie first
came on the scene.'

'But we were good for each other!' Simone
cried. 'You know we were. Everyone said so!'

'Everyone was wrong. There is only one woman
in this life who means anything and everything to
me.'

'She'll never be your equal,' Simone hissed.
'*Never!*'

Ryan turned slightly, although his eyes were
wary and didn't shift as he instructed quietly,
'Jenkins, escort Miss Vesey from the house, and
ensure that she doesn't set foot in it again.'

'Yessir! It will be a pleasure.'

'You can't do this to me!'

'I just have, Simone.'

Jenkins stepped forward and took her arm,
leading her across the pebbled courtyard, and
Natalie watched until they disappeared indoors.

'Did she harm you in any way?'

Dear Lord! Invidious words, a slap that had
almost rocked her from her feet? 'I'm all right,' she
managed quietly, aware that Ryan had moved to
stand in front of her.

'Are you?' His voice was faintly sceptical, and
her eyelids instinctively lowered as he lifted her
chin. 'Look at me, Natalie.'

Slowly she opened her eyes, meeting and

holding his gaze, and swallowed convulsively as he gently brushed his fingers over her cheek. 'You're home early.' She had to say something, otherwise she would burst into stupid childish tears.

His smile did strange things to her equilibrium, and some of the compelling formidability left his features. 'Is that all you have to say?'

'I'm temporarily lost for words.'

Gently he bent his head down to hers and trailed his lips over her cheek. 'Martha rang me,' he said close to her mouth.

'She did?'

His lips teased a trail along her jaw and sought an earlobe. 'Uh-huh. Both she and Jenkins are very protective of their ewe lamb.'

'Oh.'

His mouth closed over hers in a gentle provocative gesture, seeking an elusive response she was at that moment unable to give, and he reluctantly lifted his head.

'Neither of them were prepared to stand by and see Simone make another attempt to wreck our marriage.'

More than anything Natalie wanted to fling herself into his arms and have them hold her close. 'How much did you overhear?' she ventured at last, and glimpsed a faint speculative gleam in the eyes that surveyed her.

'Why? What did you say to her?'

Natalie felt oddly inarticulate. 'Simone did most of the talking.'

'While you sat in docile silence?'

'Not—exactly,' she conceded, fixing her gaze on the uppermost button of his black silk shirt.

'But you don't want to tell me, is that it?'

Something in his voice made her look at him, and she slowly shook her head—not in negation, but as a gesture of self-mockery at her lack of perception. 'I don't want to play games any more,' she began a trifle sadly, and his eyes narrowed fractionally.

'What are you talking about?'

'You and me,' she stated simply.

'Elaborate, Natalie,' he bade after a measurable silence, and her grey eyes were remarkably clear as she held his gaze.

'I'm tired of pretending.'

'Ah, I see.'

'Do you?'

'Shall we go inside?' he countered, and she raised her hand in an impotent gesture.

'We can talk here.'

A warm smile curved his generous mouth, reaching up to his eyes so that they crinkled with silent laughter. 'I don't imagine the *talking* will last very long. Do you want to shock the neighbours?'

'It's the middle of the afternoon,' Natalie protested, and he gave a deep throaty laugh.

'Do you want to mete out some sort of punishment by making me wait until tonight?'

'Would you?'

He reached out and tilted her chin. 'If you asked me.'

Her lower lip began to tremble. 'I love you. I never stopped.'

'I know,' Ryan said gently.

'I wanted to hurt you, the way *I* was hurt.'

'It's past, darling. Between us, we'll ensure that it never happens again.' He placed a brief hard kiss on her upturned mouth, then bent to bestow a more lingering caress before fitting her into the curve of his shoulder and leading her indoors. 'We have each other. Michelle is a bonus.'

A tiny secret smile curved her lips. 'How would you view an extra bonus?'

His glance speared her guileless features. 'Are you trying to tell me something?'

'I think I'm going to have another child,' she said quietly.

His eyes darkened measurably, and his voice sounded slightly strained. 'Do you mind?'

'Do you?' she countered slowly.

'How can you ask that?' Ryan demanded huskily as he swept her into his arms to carry her effortlessly up the stairs to their room.

Gently he lowered her to her feet, then cupped her face so that she had to look at him. 'I should have been more careful.'

'Why?' she asked simply, and saw a muscle tense along his jaw.

'You had a difficult time with Michelle.'

'Just holding her in my arms made it all worth while,' Natalie ventured quietly. 'A warm living being conceived out of love—yours and mine.'

'You're beautiful, do you know that?' he groaned emotively, and his hands slid up to her temples to hold her head. 'Will you stay with me, sleep with me, and share the rest of the days of my life?'

An impish desire to tease him a little got the better of her. 'Only the *days*, Ryan?'

'Wretch,' he laughed with glittering warmth. 'I should make you pay for that!'

'Mmm,' she whispered pensively, running the edge of her tongue along her lower lip in a deliberately provocative gesture. 'That sounds promising.'

Emotion flared in the dark golden eyes above her own, then his mouth was on hers, possessing it with a deep consuming passion that had her clinging to him unashamedly.

Slowly and with infinite gentleness he undressed

her, smiling as she helped him remove his clothes, then together they reached for each other, delighting in a mutual exploratory pleasure of all the tantalising sensory nerve-ends until only total possession could ease their aching need.

Afterwards, they rose from the bed and bathed together, then, clothed they emerged from the room and descended the stairs, arm in arm.

Natalie leaned her head momentarily against Ryan's hard shoulder and felt the answering pressure as his hand curved over her hip. She felt warm and infinitely loved, and she gave a soft bubbly laugh and raised her face for the kiss he bent low to bestow, exulting in the passion she knew would remain with them for the rest of their lives. At last, all the shadows of yesterday were gone.

A WORD ABOUT THE AUTHOR

Helen Bianchin confesses that she is torn between her allegiance to New Zealand and her fondness for Australia. She was born in New Zealand, where she lives today. But it was during an extended "working holiday" in Australia that she met her husband-to-be, Danilo.

Helen and her traveling companion had made Cairns, in northern Queensland, one of their stops. And it was while she was working for the Tobacco Association fifty miles away that she met Danilo, an Italian immigrant employed on a tobacco farm. He spoke little English. Helen's Italian was nil. But eight weeks after they met, he proposed.

It was after the birth of her third child that Helen thought seriously about writing. Her first try produced a romance novel that was too short; her second version was too long. "So," she says, "I took a deep breath, began pruning, and once again the typewriter came out and I began retyping."

Helen Bianchin's first Harlequin was *Bewildered Haven* (Romance #2010). It was published in 1976, and her typewriter has not been put away since.